I0653630

RETURN OF THE CREATORS

James Marsden

Published by New Generation Publishing in 2012

Copyright © James Marsden 2012

First Edition

The author asserts the moral right under the Copyright, Designs and Patents Act 1988 to be identified as the author of this work.

All Rights reserved. No part of this publication may be reproduced, stored in a retrieval system or transmitted, in any form or by any means without the prior consent of the author, nor be otherwise circulated in any form of binding or cover other than that which it is published and without a similar condition being imposed on the subsequent purchaser.

www.newgeneration-publishing.com

 New Generation Publishing

PROLOGUE

The discovery in 2107, during a routine blood biochemistry screening, that an eight year old boy born of an Arabic father and South American Indian mother, living on a reservation in New Mexico had an unique genetical configuration and abnormally high levels of the neurotransmitter serotonin resulted in geneticist Sam Smith head of the Human Genetic Materials Research Unit at Oxford, being charged with the investigation of the boy's genome, and associated mental abilities.

Following eighteen months of investigations, and the discovery that the boy Daniel, possessed unique psychokinetic and telekinetic abilities, Daniel disappeared from Sam's home in Valencia leaving a note saying that, by psychoportation, he was with the mythical alien race known as the Anunnaki from the planet Nibiru. From what Daniel subsequently learnt, the Anunnaki had first visited the earth some 450,000 years earlier, and with further periodic visits, had last visited the planet 4,500 years ago. They were now planning on making a return visit to Earth and were anxious to learn of the development and nature of present-day human society.

RETURN OF THE CREATORS records the events following Daniel's disappearance, his eventual return to Sam and his partner Margaret, and the events that followed which culminated in the visitation to earth by the Anunnaki – the creators of human kind.

CHAPTER ONE

The early morning sun streamed between the partly drawn curtains of Sam and Margaret's bedroom glinting on the digital clock that stood on the bedside cabinet, revealing that it was 800 hours on Saturday the 12th of May 2112. The bedroom itself formed part of the two bedroom apartment which Sam and Margaret had occupied for the last twenty years and which, between 2108 and the latter part of 2110, they had shared with a young orphaned boy Daniel Da Silva who they had adopted following the death of his parents early in 2108.

The apartment, situated on the top floor of an executive block in Valencia, had been Sam and Margaret's home since they first met through their work in human genetics, Margaret as a geneticist at the European centre for human organ replacement which was based in Valencia and where organ grafts were grown to order to be genetically compatible with the recipient, and Sam as Director of the Genetic Materials Research Unit located a few miles outside Oxford.

Sam was of average build with grey hair, a neatly trimmed white beard, white bushy eyebrows and sparkling blue eyes. His skin bronzed by the Valencia sun was wrinkle-free despite his official date of birth, which appeared in the World Population Register, being the 28 January 2001 which made him 107 at his last birthday. His ageless appearance was due to the fact that in 2041at the age of forty, he was amongst the first to volunteer to undergo the then pioneering technique of genetically switching off the ageing gene resulting in the aging process discontinuing and his remaining at that age for the foreseeable future. This technique had, in Sam's case been completely successful with both his anatomical and physiological characteristics remaining those of a man in his prime.

Easing his legs from under the duvet and slipping his feet into the slippers that were always left on his side of the bed, Sam quietly padded his way to the adjoining en-suite bathroom making sure not to disturb Margaret whose steady breathing told him that she was still asleep. After a quick shower, Sam slipped out of the bedroom into the central hallway, pausing, as he had done every morning over the past eighteen months, at the door of the second bedroom that Daniel had occupied until his disappearance eighteen months previously. During those intervening months the room had remained exactly as Daniel had left it with the note that he had written before leaving still on the bedside table. This morning, as on hundreds of previous occasions, Sam entered the room and picking up the note read once again what Daniel had penned in his script-like writing.

"Darling Aunty Margaret and Uncle Sam, Adapa came and told me that Anu wanted to see me and wanted my assistance in learning about the world of today. I shall be away for some time and can't tell you for how long, but he told me to tell you that one day I shall return and be your son again. Love always, Daniel. P.S. Give my love to Professor Regina"

As on all previous occasions there were tears in Sam's eyes as he replaced the note on the bedside table and quietly withdrew from the room which in some way had become a shrine to both Margaret and himself during the past months- a shrine that represented the only point of contact that they had with the *other world* that Daniel was now in.

Having poured himself the customary glass of orange juice from the refrigerator, Sam walked into the spacious lounge and opening the patio doors strolled into the sun bathed balcony of the penthouse apartment that overlooked the city whose origins dated back to the Bronze Age and founded by the Romans in 138 BC.

Although the old familiar landmarks of the Cathedral, the Palau de la Generalitat, the Bullring, the Valldigna Gate and the Lonja Market were still in evidence, their original usage had long since gone, although the Cathedral was still open and used by some members of the older generation who had held on to then faith that they had known in their childhood. Towering above these old buildings were the new glass and steel apartment blocks, the Education and Cultural Centre, the European Health Screening Unit with its adjoining Organ Replacement Centre, where he and Margaret had first met. In the distance was the outline of one of the world's largest Aquaria and Art Centre of which the region was very proud.

Gazing across this familiar landscape, Sam, as he had on many previous occasions, recalled the events of the last two years, events that although still secret to the population at large had stunned those members of the scientific world who had been privy to the information that Sam and his colleagues had uncovered during their studies of the genetical makeup of this young boy, and the effects that such a genetical makeup had on his mental attributes and abilities.

He recalled his initial visit as head of the Human Genetic Material Research Unit to Albuquerque, New Mexico, and to reservation 229 following a report that during the routine health screening programme of the population a young boy had been identified as having exceptional high levels of the neurotransmitter serotonin linked with all the indications that he possessed exceptional talents and mental abilities.

He recalled his very first meeting with Daniel, and of the impact this olive skinned, dark haired boy with large dark brown eyes and an engaging smile, had on him, and how he had taken an immediate personal liking to eight year old.

He also recalled the investigative work that followed, the identification of hitherto undiscovered combination of genes on chromosomes 4 and 17, chromosomes that were themselves unique to human kind, the identification of a hitherto undiscovered variant-type of the neurotransmitter serotonin, and by Neuroimaging its distribution in the brain, which in turn, was responsible for Daniel's various psychokinetic, telekinetic and teleportation abilities. These abilities had resulted in his eventual communication with *beings* from a different time and space and through psychoportation had resulted in his disappearance into their world, and the note promising a return.

Sam's thoughts were interrupted by a sleepy looking Margaret emerging onto the balcony, with the traditional glass of freshly squeezed orange juice in one hand and a copy of the weekly local news bulletin in the other. As always she wanted to know what he was thinking about, although she instinctively knew that it would be of Daniel and when he would return.

Margaret at the age of forty three years was a slim olive skinned woman with black shoulder length hair and large brown eyes that were for ever smiling. These physical attributes together with her calm and generous nature and above average intellect was what had attracted Sam to her all those years ago, and attraction that still burned brightly as she came up close and on tiptoe kissed him on the mouth.

Although they had been together approaching fifteen years, they had decided at the outset of their relationship not to have a child, which in the case of mainstream society outside reservations, was by In-Vitro-Fertilization (IVF) followed by nine months In-Vitro-Embryology (IVE), thereby allowing close genetical monitoring of the embryo, with the mother's activities not restricted due to pregnancy. The genetical monitoring of children born by this method ensured that any genetical abnormalities could be removed or suppressed at a very early stage and that the children had attributes considered desirable by their biological parents and society in general. In addition, a process of programmed engineering ensured that and talents and abilities that their genome would contain was related to their prospects in those work areas relative to the needs of society at that time.

This "designer-baby" concept was in Margaret's view an unacceptable aspect of mainstream society, although children of poor parenting in the early and middle part of the 21st century had caused much disruption and social conflict. Margaret viewed the bringing up of a child by caring and responsible parents in a loving home as the basis of parenthood and the wish to have a child. It was this unshakable conviction that had made their decision to adopt Daniel, following the tragic death of his parents, that much easier, with Margaret's willingness to take indefinite sabbatical leave from her work as a geneticist, a determining factor in Daniel's development during the two years in Valencia.

His disappearance eighteen months previous had consequently had a devastating effect on Margaret, and every day she, like Sam, checked his bedroom hoping that she would find him back safely in his bed and with his adopted family, while every evening before retiring,

8

she prayed for the safe   return of the young boy who had filled an hitherto void in her otherwise happy and contented life.

When would he return? What would he be able to tell them? Would the Anunnaki be pleased with what he could tell them of humanity in the 22nd century? These were all questions that both Margaret and Sam hoped that Daniel would be able to answer upon his return.

CHAPTER TWO

The report that Sam had submitted to the World Genetics Centre in Brisbane Australia outlining the contact that Daniel had established with Adapa and then with one of his Anunnaki creators Anu, had brought an instant response from its Director Mark Andrews, since this first known contact between a human being and an extraterrestrial had enormous implications both scientifically and socially.

The fact that this contact was supported by a micro-disc which portrayed, through a brain-recording made at the time, of what Daniel had seen during his psychoportation to the space ship of the Anunnaki, was of immense importance, while equally startling was the timing of these events which, if Zecharia Sitchin's research carried out in the 20th century and recorded in his book *The Earth Chronicles* was found to be correct, was exactly one hundred years later than his prediction that the planet Nibiru would be at its nearest point to Earth in 2012.

When Sam's report was followed few days later by the news that Daniel had gone on a further psychoportation trip of indeterminate length, Sam was immediately summoned to Brisbane for a top security briefing.

Landing at Brisbane airport, Sam had been whisked away in the personal transport of Mark Andrews to a meeting with Mark and Andrew Shafter the World Government Minister with responsibility for World Population trends and Development, who had been involved with Daniel's case since its inception. Both men had greeted Sam warmly, and following some light refreshments and the usual small talk, which centred around Margaret and how she was coping with Daniel's disappearance, the three men had got down to assessing the situation, what the outcome and its implications might be.

Top of the agenda had been how Daniel's sudden disappearance could be explained to his friends and neighbours, since such an event with no prior warning might result in some well meaning person reporting the incident to the authorities.

The second topic related to what information Daniel was likely to pass-on to the Anunnaki in the context of his outstanding learning abilities, retention of knowledge, and those learning experiences that both Sam and Margaret had introduced him to, over the last eighteen months. Finally, there had been the discussion as to whether the train of events that had culminated in the Anunnaki or Nibiruans as they were sometimes known making contact with Daniel as a consequence of his special powers, was a prelude to the Anunnaki making a return visit to Earth, after an interval of around 4,500 years.

Whereas the cover story for Daniel's disappearance from his home in Valencia, was one that was fairly easy to concoct, and would be based on some distant relatives of his late mother and father, currently living in New Mexico, inviting him to their home on an extended stay. An invitation that Sam and Margaret had welcomed since it would give Daniel a better understanding of his "roots".

What information Daniel would divulge to the Anunnaki was anybody's guess, since all three men were aware that Daniel's ability to absorb knowledge was phenomenal, and that together with his experiences in visiting the locations of the earliest civilizations recorded on earth, coupled with what Sam and Margaret had explained to him about human society at the beginning of the 22nd century, Daniel would be well equipped to answer most questions relating to the stages in the development of human society, the various mechanisms that had been introduced to bring about World Government, the reduction in inherited diseases and antisocial behaviour patterns through genetic engineering, and the containment of the ever present tendency for conflict between ethnic and religious groups.

In relation to the possible link between the planet Nibiru on its 4,500 year orbit round the sun, and Daniel's contact with extraterrestrials, the scientific evidence obtained from the space scientists was that this planet, whose very existence had only been confirmed in 2083, although its presence had been identified by the Sumerians some 5,000 years previously, would be at its nearest point to Earth some time during 2112, although due to its elliptical orbit an exact calculation had proved difficult.

The final discussions revolved around the need to continue with Sam's investigation of Daniel's genome and in particular the 453 identified genes on chromosome 4, and the 1,367 identified genes on chromosome 17. These two chromosome pairs were themselves unique to humans and did not appear in any other species of *primate,* and were in all probability originally from the "gene bank" of the Anunnaki and introduced during the creation process of mankind.

The replication, and possible re-introduction of some if not all of these genes into the human genome was of immense importance in the future development of humans and a major step towards *Tran humanisation.*

This task Sam had been happy to comply with, since following his indefinite sabbatical leave as Director of the Genetics Materials Centre, to care for Daniel and to visit the ancient sites of early civilisations, the boy's disappearance after eighteen months had left a great void in his life and time had lain heavily on his hands.

Sam was also very aware that the same applied to Margaret, so before returning to Valencia he had arranged for her to have the option of returning to work at the European centre for human organ replacement until such time as Daniel would return.

Upon his return to Valencia, Sam outlined the topics discussed at the Brisbane meeting and of the recommendations made in respect of his ongoing work at Oxford, and the suggestion that Margaret should suspend her sabbatical leave and return to work until such time as Daniel returned. Although she would never openly admit to welcoming this suggestion, she was secretly pleased with the suggestion since anything that would occupy her mind until the return of the boy who she regarded as her own son, would help.

She also wanted to know what Sam's opinion was in relation to further identification of the individual genes or aggregate of genes that had resulted in Daniel's special abilities, and of the possibility of replicating individual genes for introduction into other human genomes. Finally, and in true Margaret-style, she promised Sam that she would prepare a list of the most important changes in human society over the last 100 years in the hope that one day she could compare this with the information that Daniel would have given to the Anunnaki.

CHAPTER THREE

The months following Sam's visit to Brisbane were relatively uneventful. Margaret returned to work at the European Centre for Human Organ Replacement, while Sam returned to Oxford and to his private laboratory at the Human Genetic Material Research Unit, returning to Valencia every weekend to be with Margaret and to recall happier days when Daniel had been the focus of their lives.

True to her word Margaret had spent much of her spare-time outside work listing the major changes that had occurred in society over the last hundred years, while at the same time attempting to give rational reasons for such changes, which in the main, and in her opinion, were due to the genetical traits of humans which had been present in their *primate ancestors* who themselves had evolved by natural selection over millions of years, and which the Anunnaki, despite their skill at genetical engineering, had been unable to eradicate completely.

These traits, while crucial to the survival of the original *primate* species were completely inappropriate in what could be termed a civilised society and despite the efforts of the Anunnaki during their various return visits to earth, to educate and guide the various human populations in the ways of an organised and civilised society, these traits continued to be the Achilles Heel of modern man.

Recalling what Adapa had told Daniel of the initial problems that the Anunnaki had encountered during the creation of man, those traits, that still exist in modern *Primates* such as the great apes and chimpanzees, appeared to be the most difficult to eradicate through genetical engineering. These included tribal attributes consistent with the need for collective protection;

aggressive behaviour patterns also a pre-requisite for survival, sexual drive and the need to propagate the species, and personal greed.

When applied to the earliest known civilisations such as the Sumerians, and later the Egyptians, and the Mayans of South America, there was little doubt in Margaret's mind that these ancient civilisations had, at some time in their past, benefited from guidance from the Anunnaki, and that such civilisations continued to copy what they recalled, through their genetic memories and cultures, of the activities of their creators.

An example of such recall being the Egyptians using pyramid chambers as burial sites for their pharaohs, since memories recalled the link between pyramids, birth and creation as performed by the Anunnaki, and the transfer of individuals to another world or to the after-life.

Likewise the cave systems in South America representing "Chicomoztoc" was, according to the mythology of the Chichimec people, where their ancestors were believed to have been created and first emerged onto the earth.

This guidance however had a very limited effect on inherent tribal attitudes with the separation of the warring fractions being the only viable long- term solution.

Through genetic *labelling* involving 1% of the total genome, physical characteristics that made them identifiable from each other and to the Anunnaki was achieved, and the populations so identified were separated geographically, giving rise to the seven macro ethnicity groupings and the 52 micro ethnicity groups that still occupy specific global regions.

Superimposed on this ethnicity and geographical separation was the teachings of the Anunnaki, that over the millennia, evolved as the basis of the various religions of the world, and that despite the passage of time, were all based on belief that at some time in the past *Gods* (The Anunnaki) descended from heaven, created man, and gave him basic rules of self and social behaviour, and that one day the *Gods* would return.

From Margaret's knowledge of more recent history there was little doubt in her mind that throughout time conflict within the human race was rooted in either ethnic or religious grounds with aggressive tendencies, personal and "national" greed, and the search for power being additional factors. Traditional wars were mainly fought between groups or "nations" of different ethnic backgrounds, with the objective of gaining territory and wealth, or as in the case of the holy wars, fought by the Crusaders, based on religious beliefs as well as ethnic differences.

Although the major wars of the 20th century such as the 1st and 2nd World Wars related to ethnic origins and culture and the quest for world domination, other more minor wars, such as the Korean and Vietnamese wars, had much to do with political ideology, while the Iraq Wars at the end of the 20th century were basically the protection of the world's most valuable natural energy resource – namely oil.

The two most significant developments of the 20th and 21st centuries were, in Margaret's view, inexpensive means of travel and the development of the World Web. These developments resulted in humans through the web having access to world-wide information not previously easily available, while inexpensive air travel provided the means by which world travel was possible to individuals and families.

In terms of timing these developments occurred when high levels of economic inequality existed between the different regions and nations of the world, and consequently resulted in mass economic migration from the poor to the more prosperous countries. Such economic migration occurred, and was allowed to occur by national governments, with little consideration as to the ethnic or religious background of the immigrants involved, resulting in countries with long established traditional and valued cultures, finding their culture replaced by a multicultural one.

Although these changes were initially tolerated by the indigenous ethnic population, by the middle of the 21st century a turn-down in the global economy resulted in wide spread unrest and conflict between religious and ethnic groups, much of which being the result of religious teachings far removed from the initial religious concept, which in all religions emphasised the need to love one's fellow human being, and the return of poor employment prospects with the migrants of different ethnic origins acquiring employment at the expense of the indigenous population.

Another major development in the late 20th and early 21st century was the emergence of the Global Economy with International and Multi-National Companies having the power to switch their activities world wide for purely economic reasons and with no reference to any National Government. This development, together with the emergence of Global Money Markets and the power of the media resulted in the autonomy of the Nation-State being eroded to such an extent as to be completely ineffective.

These developments and their combined effects had a cataclysmic influence on democratically elected National Governments whose ability to govern had been dramatically reduced. This in turn had led to politicians making promises that they had little or no chance of keeping, resulting in a sharp decline in political awareness and interest, with politicians being regarded as false and unworthy of the peoples' trust.

Against this background of events, and after the initial establishment of five major geographical governments namely – North and South America, European, Chinese, Indian and Australasia, their combination to form a world government was inevitable, with this occurring in the year 2085.

It was only as a result of the establishment of this World Government consisting of highly intelligent and motivated individuals who considered world interests as being above national interests, that the events over the next thirty years had been possible, events that Margaret had grown up with, and which she had outlined to Daniel on numerous occasions.

It was at this point that Margaret decided that a summary of the developments in world society over the past thirty years would best be left until she could seek Sam's advice on the order of importance and relevance of these more recent developments.

CHAPTER FOUR

The following weekend, after Margaret had acquainted Sam of what she had been doing in her spare time and showed him her neatly presented copy of events that had culminated in the establishment of a World Government, they were soon immersed in discussions relating to developments that had occurred world-wide since 2085, and the relative importance of such developments.

In keeping with his long term interest in human genetics, his work at the Oxford unit, the fact that he himself was a product of genetic engineering that had enabled his aging process to be stopped at the age of forty, and now his ongoing work on Daniel's genome, Sam viewed the establishment of the World Genetics Centre, the DNA screening of the world's population, the establishment of an ongoing programme of in-vitro fertilization (IVF) and in-vitro embryological development (IVE) that allowed for the enhancement of the genetic profile of future generations, and the genetic tailoring of the individual's genome to occupational interests, as being the most important developments of the last few decades.

However, as he admitted to Margaret, a great deal of the technology associated with such genetic screening, the identification of specific disease carrying genes, their subsequent elimination, and the concept of designer children, had been developed well before 2085, although up until that date, National Governments had shied away from total support for such screening due to being afraid of the information being used for ethnic cleansing purposes, and bringing about even greater conflict to multicultural societies.

In actual fact however, compulsory genetic screening and clear   definitions of ethnicity had brought about numerous unanticipated benefits, since with the different regions of the world achieving economic comparability through strong world governance, those identified as belonging to the various ethnic groupings actively supported a return to their ancestral homelands.

This unanticipated development resulted in the repatriation policy being very much easier to implement with the once poorer and under populated regions that had suffered due to earlier economic migration, benefiting by this return of its people.

Whilst accepting the importance of this 21st century development, Margaret viewed the removal of the Global Money Markets, made non-viable by the introduction of a single world-wide currency, the establishment of a profit limit on all trading, which effectively removed the "greed factor" and dedication to "profits at all costs" from industry and commerce, the demise of the multi-national company and the evolution of "regional" industry and commerce, as being of equal importance, and instrumental in the economic equalisation of the different regions of the globe.

She also viewed the element of choice that had been introduced into an otherwise highly regulated society as being of great importance. In particular Type 2 Reservations where those wishing to follow a more traditional pattern of family life outside mainstream society could still do so, although as in keeping with main stream society, the number of children that traditional parents could have were restricted, as was travel outside the reservation area. Such reservations also provided, through their programmes of health and genetic screening, invaluable information in terms of genetic material as exemplified by the discovery of Daniel's unique genome and abilities.

The removal world-wide of prisons, young offenders' institutions, and similar detention facilities, to be replaced by Type 1 Reservations providing a more natural and humane environment was also, in Margaret's opinion of enormous importance. With their own infrastructure, security and services, these reservations required all inmates to work during their stay, be screened for genetic traits which could be related to their criminal activities and anti-social behaviour, while at the same time being subjected to training programmes aimed at the correction of existing behaviour patterns.

Security on Type 1 reservations was tight, with all inmates electronically "tagged", and with movement strictly restricted to the confines of the reservation. Possible eventual transfer to Type 2 reservations was only implemented after extensive long-term monitoring of behaviour patterns, with the average stay on the reservation being from three to five years with the most serious crimes resulting in an indefinite stay.

In terms of the personal finance of the individual living in main stream society, the removal of the credit card system, which had resulted in much human misery, and its replacement by a "personal funding" card, which made spending levels above the ability to pay impossible, was a major step towards the financial education of society as a whole.

Linked to this development was the establishment of a world-wide wages and personal taxation structure linked to type and levels of responsibility and with no differentiation between male and female workers.

This development in turn had removed the incentive for economic migration, which in the past, had been due mainly to inequality of earnings and benefits across the world.

The final important development, which both Sam and Margaret agreed upon, was the replacement of fossil fuels as a source of energy by the development of solar and the hydrogen cell. The latter revolutionised the supply of energy for industry, business, commerce and equally important, all forms of transport. With the only bi-product of this energy generating process being water, the on-going need to control, and if possible curtail, global warming, was greatly enhanced.

Due to the development of a hydrogen powered integrated system of public transport the need for private or personal transport was greatly reduced and the grid-locked cities of the 21st century were a thing of the past, while the regionalisation of society's needs in terms of food and clothing and energy, meant that food and clothing products were not transported half-way round the world as had occurred in the early and middle part of the 21st century, but were provided from within the various global regions.

As Sam and Margaret recapped on their list of developments and achievements attributable to mankind they realised that the relatively recent concepts developed by World Government had numerous similarities to the approach taken by the Anunnaki in their quest for the civilisation of their creation some 450,000 years previously.

At this stage Sam also realised that one other similarity with the Anunnaki that he and Margaret had erroneously left off their list, related to space exploration and space travel, which although still in its infancy despite 150 years of development, was an attempt by humans to replicate the space-travel capabilities of their creators as portrayed in the cultural myths and religions of humanity.

CHAPTER FIVE

Having completed their list of developments, which they hoped one day they would be able to discuss with Daniel, in the context of what information the Anunnaki were seeking, Sam and Margaret settled down to enjoy each others company for the remainder of the weekend, since despite their twenty plus years together they still loved each other with a passion that had remained unabated over the years.

All too soon the weekend was over and Monday morning saw Margaret setting off for work at the European centre for human organ replacement, while Sam took the short journey to Valencia airport where, as was normal, his X33 space plane powered by eco-friendly hydrogen was ready to take him to London and his research laboratory at Oxford.

Following the decision of the World Genetics Centre that Sam be given indefinite sabbatical leave from his post as Director of the Human Genetic Materials research Unit, in order to devote his time to bringing up his now adopted son Daniel, and to further research the boy's unique genome, biochemical profile and psychokinetic, telekinetic and psychoportation abilities, Dr Edward Chapman had been seconded from Oxford's sister-unit in North America, and appointed as acting Director of the Oxford Unit.

Like Sam he had benefited from having his ageing-gene suppressed ten years earlier and with a biological age of forty Edward Chapman was a tall athletic dark haired man of a serious disposition, whose one shortcoming, in Sam's opinion, was his rather inflated sense of his own importance, which over the last eighteen months had caused some friction between him and some of his colleagues at the unit.

This friction had been particularly noticeable in his dealings with Paul and Julie who had worked closely with Sam on what had become known within the unit, as the "Daniel Project", and although well aware that the project had been given the highest security classification, with details only known to Mark Andrews Director of the World Genetics Centre, Sam, and to a much lesser extent Julie and Paul, this restriction appeared to grate with Edward Chapman who felt that as acting Director he should also be given full details.

Since Daniel's disappearance and his meeting in Brisbane, Sam had thrown himself into working on Daniel's genome in the hope of discovering further hitherto unknown combinations of genes on Chromosomes 4 and 17 and possible reasons for the rearrangement of around 100,000 DNA base pairs from chromosome 1 to the male Y chromosome.

In particular Sam's research concentrated on identifying the number of protein-encoding genes on these particular chromosomes, since it was the discovery of one such protein-encoding gene responsible for the production of a variant form of serotonin in Daniel's brain that, in turn had led to his psychoportation, psychokinetic and telekinetic abilities and his ability to communicate with the extraterrestrial Anunnaki.

One of the many problems that Sam had faced during this research was due to many protein-encoding genes producing more than one protein, with on average each gene producing 2 to 3 different proteins. This feature had been exemplified by the encoding gene producing Daniel's serotonin producing both the normal type and the variant type which had an entirely different effect on the functioning of the brain cells.

Added to this major problem was the fact that in the human genome there are a large proportion of *control* genes or *enhancers* which give the protein-encoding genes greater flexibility. It was the discovery of these *enhancers* and the means by which they could be modified chemically during embryological development that had enabled geneticists to "block" many of the genes that gave rise to genetical abnormalities such as Down's syndrome, Wolf-Hirsch-horn syndrome, Edward's syndrome, Jacobsen syndrome Turner syndrome and the like, and retard such conditions as Parkinson's disease, Multiple sclerosis, Alzheimer's and most importantly of all, the ageing process in selected individuals.

There was also gene diversity and density with the average human gene containing 4 *exons* each consisting of around 338 base pairs and capable of encoding a protein of 450 amino-acids. The density of genes on the different chromosomes also varies ranging from 23 genes per million base pairs to 5 genes per million base pairs.

Until the advent of gene chip technology such analysis of human chromosomes had not been possible, and although the Human Genome Project had been in existence since the early part of the 21st century, the exact number of genes in the human genome was still a matter for debate and had still to be finalised.

Sam's work in relation to Daniel's genome however, had concentrated on a relatively small part of the genome- namely those encoding genes and their *enhancers* that occurred on chromosomes 4 and 17 which themselves were unique to humans and did not appear in any other species of *primate*.

This work was highly complex since it involved introducing Daniel's DNA into e-nucleated human stem-cells, allowing several stages of cell division to occur and then when the encoding genes synthesised proteins, analysing the protein structure for variation in the amino acid configuration and comparing such configuration with a known "normal". Although the work that Sam had pursued since Daniel's disappearance had only revealed two abnormal configurations in addition to the variant serotonin, he was well pleased by these results, while the work itself made him feel close to the boy who had effectively changed his life.

As Sam entered the Unit on that Monday morning, he was greeted by Edward Chapman who appeared in high spirits and invited him for morning coffee before he started work. As always, Sam was cautious of this approach, and such cautiousness was soon justified by Edward wanting to know how Daniel was, and had he made much progress in his research. While being polite, Sam was careful in what was said and soon made his excuses to curtail the conversation, leaving with a nagging question at the back of his mind as to why Edward Chapman appeared to be so interested in the "Daniel Project".

Making his way to his office adjoining research laboratory that had been set aside for his own private use, Sam called in to see Paul whose expertise in the biochemical analysis of proteins he had always rated highly, and whose work with Daniel at both the University of California and at the London Medical Centre had resulted in the breakthrough of relating a specific encoding gene, to a variant form of serotonin whose action in the brain resulted in his developing the ability to communicate with extraterrestrials and through psychoportation have the ability to visit a different time and space.

As always Paul was pleased to see Sam and always asked about Daniel, since although he was aware of the boy's unique abilities he was unaware of Daniel's disappearance, accepting that he was on an extended visit to some recently discovered relatives in New Mexico.

As Sam entered his office his desk qPhone was blinking warning him that he had a call and one that was using a high security frequency. Picking up the qPhone Sam was surprised to hear Margaret's familiar voice at the other end since it was only in an emergency that she ever contacted him at work. What was the problem? Was she alright? These were questions that sprang to Sam's mind? Her voice husky with excitement Margaret whispered three words- "Daniel is back".

CHAPTER SIX

Within three hours Sam was in the lift taking him to his penthouse home in Valencia, a home that he had only left a few hours earlier. As he watched the floor indicator on the lift climb ever upwards Sam could but wonder if Daniel's experiences over the last eighteen months had in any way changed him, would he still be the young man who he and Margaret had adopted and taken to their hearts, what knowledge had he acquired from the Anunnaki, and equally important what knowledge had they acquired from him? Sam's thoughts were interrupted by the bell that announced that he had arrived on the top floor.

Slipping his key-card into the lock, Sam eased open the door, and as was his custom gave a whistle to announced his return. Within seconds the lounge door burst open and in a blur of arms and legs Daniel launched himself into his arms. "I'm back Uncle Sam, I have so much to tell you, and I love you very much". As Sam untangled himself from Daniel's arms and stepped back to have a good look at him, Margaret emerged from the kitchen with her face writhed in a smile that he had not seen for the last eighteen months. "Well what do you think of him, he's grown don't you think?" she asked.

Looking down at the olive skinned, black haired boy with his large brown eyes and engaging smile, Sam realised how much he had missed the boy, who although having only entered their lives four short years previously, had completely changed their priorities for ever.

Following the meal that Margaret had prepared in her usual skilled way, and which Daniel tackled with great enthusiasm, commenting that it was the best since he left, all three retired to the lounge, and although Sam was very aware that he should be contacting Brisbane to report Daniel's return, he viewed quality time with the boy as being more important, and although not wishing to pressurise the boy in any way he viewed that knowing what had transpired during the past eighteen months that Daniel had been with the Anunnaki, as being the top priority.

With a recording device in place, Daniel commenced what was to be the very first account of the creation and development of humankind on the earth as told by a member of the Anunnaki race and the creators of humankind. This unique communication being possible through Daniel's ESP and teleportation abilities, which in turn were the result of his unique genome and those genes implanted by the Anunnaki 450,000 years previous. .As on previous occasions, it all started one night when he was woken by Adapa standing by his bed, and through their special form of ESP communication, telling him that he had come to take him to Anu who wanted to see and talk to him about the past, present, and future of human kind. Since this would take considerable time Adapa had told him that he should leave a short message for Sam and Margaret explaining his disappearance, and then prepare himself for the various stages of psychoportation that Adapa had guided him through on previous occasions.

On arrival on the flight deck of the space ship with its array of dials and controls and its "winged disc" symbol which, throughout mythology had been identified with the star ships of the Anunnaki, and a visual representation of the humanoid spirit's ability to fly free of the body, Daniel once again found himself face to face with the tall gaunt humanoid figure of Anu with his long blond hair, deeply tanned skin and startling blue eyes, which unlike the first occasion that they had met, now had a hint of warmth and welcome as he extended his hands to perform the touching of finger-tips which was the Anunnaki traditional form of greeting.

During the subsequent telepathic conversation Anu explained that ever since their very first visit to earth around 450,000 years previously, when they were searching for elements and minerals such as gold and jade that had been mined to exhaustion on their own planet of Nibiru, and when, in order to assist them in the mining of such materials they had genetically engineered suitable *primates* to aid them in these tasks, they had always returned when their planet, on its 4,500 year orbit of the Sun, was closest to earth, in order to ascertain the progress made by their human creation .

Unlike their first meeting, Anu was at pains to explain that although the Anunnaki were a very long-living race he had only visited the earth on the last ten occasions when the planet Nibiru was closest to the earth, and that although these visits only covered a period of 45,000 years, they did represent the most significant period of human development.

Anu then went on to explain that the Anunnaki had, during this initial visit to earth, established numerous bases, primarily in the Southern Hemisphere which at the time was unaffected by the Ice Age, and close to those regions where their "scanners" had detected mineral deposits that could be mined. Such regions included the Middle-East- Lebanon, Israel, Egypt, Iraq, India, South Africa and South America, and were subsequently identified by the Anunnaki using their advanced laser technology building large stone pyramids that were large enough to be seen from space, and which in addition to serving as "markers" to guide subsequent visitors to earth, provided the locations for the genetic engineering work aimed at generating a work force required for the mining of ores.

Anu went on identify the very first region of occupation as being in the region between the rivers Tigris and Euphrates in an area that was very much later became known as Mesopotamia. This area was particularly rich in a whole range of elements and was the area where the very first genetical experiments on indigenous *primates* were undertaken which eventually resulted in the creation of mankind.

This creation with a genome containing around 20% of DNA from the Anunnaki "genetic bank", with much of this donor DNA "blocked", due to the Anunnaki being very aware of the potential dangers that the granting of their amazing powers to an uneducated and untried species might present, and with the remainder being that of the indigenous *primate* where their attempts at eliminating many of those undesirable qualities identified, only being partly successful, made the provision of some guidelines for the species essential.

Once having created humans and having observed their development during subsequent visits to earth, the Anunnaki came to the conclusion that it was their responsibility to bring knowledge to humanity, and it was in this role as teachers that resulted in their being seen and remembered as gods instrumental in assisting humanity in acquiring a common knowledge relating to astrology, artwork, music, science, technology, social behaviour, and indeed, the knowledge of how to become human and how to take care of themselves.

It was these initial teachings that enabled humans all over the earth to establish cultures, albeit with different names depending on their location, but with all depicting stories of the gods being on ships that came from the skies, and of their gifts of knowledge to humanity. As with all teachers, they were, as Anu recalled, manipulators, and as long as humans did not upset them they were safe and provided for. But as the species evolved they began to question their purpose and their future and became discontented with their role as workers or slaves wanting to have the *nectar* of the gods for themselves.

They wanted to live as long as their gods did, and wanted their powers and wealth or whatever they felt they lacked and although much of what they wanted had been engineered into their *genome* it would be millennia later before such knowledge and power appeared at random in certain individuals, resulting in mankind making further strides towards their goal.

At this stage in his account, Daniel gave a yawn and although he had not complained, Sam and Margaret realised how true the last remarks by Anu were, and that Daniel, although having inherited many of the abilities and powers of the Anunnaki, was indeed human and not at all like his creators.

CHAPTER SEVEN

The following morning Daniel was up and about early having come into Sam and Margaret's bedroom informing them that he had experienced a wonderful night's sleep and that all the tiredness of the previous day was gone. Sam and Margaret were however somewhat jaded, had spent much of the night discussing the significance of what Daniel had recalled of his conversation with Anu, and theorising as to what other pieces of the jigsaw of human existence on earth would be revealed when he continued his astonishing account.

Immediately after breakfast Sam, using his secure mailing facility, emailed Mark Andrews informing him of Daniel's return and of the fact that he had already commenced a debriefing exercise to ascertain what information that he had been given by the Anunnaki, what information had they requested of him and to what purpose, and most important of all, if, where and when they would be returning to earth.

Following a visit to his friend Leon in the adjoining apartment to announce his return, and the usual snack lunch, Daniel was ready to continue with his account of his time in the company of the Anunnaki. With the recording device in play, Sam and Margaret settled down to listen to yet another instalment of what was by any standards an astonishing account.

According to Anu, the first visit to earth had resulted in the creation, through the genetic engineering, of human beings. Subsequent cloning, genetic refinement, and natural copulation of male and female had eventually led to the establishment of a primitive society in the region of Mesopotamia. This region at that time presented a very lush and attractive environment with fertile land perfect for growing things, a source of fresh water and a wealth of minerals and natural resources. Successive visits at around 4,500 year intervals, had however revealed that many of the characteristics that had served the *primates* well during their evolution by natural selection, were presenting problems in the fledgling human society. The natural aggressive and tribal tendencies, territorial instincts, and greed of *primates* had resulted in much conflict and death in the fledgling communities, with there being little observance and recall of the initial teachings and guidelines passed down by the creators.

These initial failures, coupled with the need to establish further mineral-rich locations across the Southern Hemisphere from the Middle East westwards across India, Africa, Atlantis, South America and China, resulted eventually in the various warring fractions being separated geographically, with "marker" genes, accounting for 1% of the total genome, being introduced into their genome to give the various groups different physical characteristics, facial appearance and skin colouring.

Against this background, and with further teachings by the Anunnaki, primitive societies were established across the Southern Hemisphere each recognisable by their physical characteristics and each provided with further guidelines for living, which once established over the millennia, gave rise to cultures and myths of the various societies, that although different in detail, had one think in common- namely, the belief in godlike- beings on ships that came from the skies and who were instrumental in the creation of humankind.

It was the wish of the Anunnaki that these beliefs would become engrained in humanity and lead to their feeling of an affinity with their creators and a belief that this initial guidance would still influence humans some 450,000 years later.

In other words, these archetypes implanted within human beings as myths and cultures would continue to help humans through life, and show them what humans were potentially capable of.

One of the most significant influences that Anunnaki teachings had on humanity was in changing the hitherto nomadic tendencies of the engineered *primate species* to acceptance, understanding and appreciation of the advantages of the static community, and its resulting development. Such development included the cultivation of land to grow crops, the herding of animals for food, and the construction of shelters for the individual and community as a whole.

Anu, as Daniel recalled, had then gone on to identify the first such settled societies to manifest those features needed to qualify as a civilization. First and foremost was the civilization established in the region known as Sumer, Sumeru or Shinar with its settlement of Eridu established after a hundred successive visits by the Anunnaki, and around 440,000 earth-years after their very first visit.

Eridu became the home of the Anunnaki culture God Enki or Ea, who was recognised as the god of beneficence, a healer and friend to humanity who gave humanity knowledge of the arts and sciences, the industries and manners of civilization, and most important of all, the first law-book. This development, according to Anu was of immense satisfaction to the Anunnaki many of whom had almost given up on ever achieving their initial objectives of a civilisation comparable to their own.

Although Eridu was the dominant centre of the fledgling civilisation there was another neighbour settlement known as Ur which was the home of another Anunnaki god Enlil, and which had originated within the region of Nippur.

35

Anu recalled that during his last visit to earth, these two cultures had coalesced, and although Eridu had remained the dominant partner, the coming together of the two societies had, once again resulted in the problem of unrest between the two fractions.

In response to Daniel wanting to know what human society was like at that time, Anu became careful in his choice of words, explaining to Daniel that it was very unlike what he had experienced in his short life, but that he was willing to outline the basic structure.

Society, according to Anu was male dominated, with a social structure consisting of the Lu-gal or head man, and with all other members belonging to one of two basic strata - the *Lu* or free person, and the *arad* (male) and the *geme* (female), who were in the main regarded as slaves. The son of a *Lu* was called a *dumu-nita* until he took a wife. A woman (*munus)* went from being a daughter (*dumu-mi)* to a wife (*dam),* then if she outlived her husband, a widow (*numasu)* who could remarry. Although initially the custom of polyandry was common with women taking multiple husbands, this was eventually discouraged in favour of the more stable monogamous partnerships.

The language used for communication was an agglutinative one where morphemes or units of meaning were added together to create words. The written word was by a system of picture-hieroglyphs that later became known as cuneiform which were recorded on clay tablets, although different objects such as bricks were subsequently used to record letters and transactions, laws, prayers, scientific texts including mathematics, astronomy and medicine.

At this point Daniel declared that he was exhausted, would like to go to bed, and would continue his account the following day. After his departure, Sam and Margaret played back some of the information given to make sure that they had not missed, or misunderstood any part of his tale.

CHAPTER EIGHT

Later that afternoon Sam received a communication from Mark Andrews acknowledging the news of Daniel's return and expressing the wish that he and Andrew Shafter the World Government Minister with responsibility for World Population Trends and Development, would like to meet Sam, Margaret and Daniel at the earliest opportunity.

Having acknowledged the communication, Sam and Margaret proceeded to consider alternative dates for such a visit, being mindful of the fact that Daniel had still to complete his account of his experiences over the last eighteen months, while Margaret would require leave of absence from her work at the European centre for human organ replacement.

When Daniel was told of their impending visit to Brisbane accompanied by both Sam and Margaret he gave a whoopee of delight recalling their previous visits to South America and the Middle East and his introduction to what remained of ancient civilisations, which as a result of his conversation with Anu, he was able to confirm as having been established initially by the Anunnaki, Nibiruans or Nefilim as mentioned in the Old Testament and translated means "those who came down".

That evening after supper and with the recording device switched on, Daniel continued with his account of how Anu had explained the temple-centered farming communities that achieved a social stability that ensured their survival over the millennia.

The Anunnaki temple-gods ruled each community organising the mass labour projects necessary for agriculture, in the same way as they had initially organised gangs of newly created and cloned humans to mine the ores that they needed. Since all such communities were located in the Southern Hemisphere just south of the equator, all forms of agriculture depended heavily on irrigation which in the main was achieved through the construction of canals, channels, dykes, weirs and reservoirs or artificial lakes. Foremost in these developments were the communities located in the region of Sumer the homeland of those humans who much later became known as Sumerians living in the region which millennia later became known as Mesopotamia.

It was also in this region that according to Anu human society was instructed in technological development and its applications that gave rise to the wheel – firstly as a potter's aid, then as a means of milling grain and later in the wheeled vehicle. Other developments included cuneiform writing, arithmetic using several different number systems, geometry, the lunisolar calendar, astronomy with the five planets that were visible to the naked eye given names, and the mapping of stars into sets of constellations, many of which survive in the astrological signs of the zodiac.

The smelting of metals such as copper and the amalgamation of different metals to form alloys such as bronze was another major development in the education of humanity. This production of metals by the smelting of ores was initially the purview of the Anunnaki using their laser technology and sophisticated laser-based equipment, and it was not until humans were instructed in the uses of fire, that their ability to manufacture saws, chisels, hammers, braces, bits, nails, pins, rings, hoes, axes, knives, swords, protective armour, war chariots, boots and sandals came about.

Another crucial development in establishing any form of recognisable civilisation was the means of recording events and information, and although initially the invention of cuneiform derived from picture-hieroglyphs, had limited usage, its development onto clay tablets resulted in personal and business letters and transactions, receipts, laws, prayers, magical incantations, and scientific texts including mathematics, astronomy, and medicine being recorded for future generations.

In terms of buildings and architecture, although the Anunnaki had used stone cut by lasers into blocks that were subsequently fitted together through their psychokinetic/telekinetic abilities, the building materials used by these early human civilisations consisted of mud brick. Such mud-brick buildings rapidly deteriorated and were periodically destroyed, levelled, and rebuilt on the same spot. This constant rebuilding gradually raised the level of settlements, so that they came to be elevated above the surrounding plain. These resultant hills known as *tells* were a feature of ancient settlements in the Middle East region.

As the architectural abilities and skills of humans progressed under the guidance of the temple-gods, they developed the arch and by constructing several arches developed a strong type of roof called a dome, and just as the Anunnaki had ensured that much of their knowledge and skills were not made known to their human prodigy, so now did those humans who had gained knowledge of architecture and building constructions, guard this information from their fellow workers, forming the beginnings of the *Masonic* movement aimed at guarding and protecting their specialist knowledge of building and construction from others.

As societies grew and spread geographically, various areas rich in certain materials started trading with adjoining areas where such resources were scarce or not available. This marked the beginnings of trading arrangements made possible by the invention and development of the boat as a means of transport. There were according to Anu three types of boat developed in this area, skin boats comprising of animal skins stretched over reeds and cane; clinker-built sailboats stitched together with hair and waterproofed with bitumen; and wooden-oared river- boats that were pulled along by people and/or animals walking along the river bank. This region with its inventions and innovations became recognised as being the birthplace of the most creative culture in human pre-history and a tribute to the teachings of the Anunnaki.

At which point, Sam switched off the recording device suggesting that tomorrow was another day - and one where arrangements for their impending visit to Brisbane would need to be finalised.

The following morning over breakfast details of the impending visit to Brisbane and the meeting with Mark Andrews and Andrew Shafter were discussed. Margaret had already informed her employer of Daniel's return and the fact that she would require further sabbatical leave, while Sam had sent a polite email to Edward Chapman, informing him out of courtesy that he would not be at the Unit for the next few weeks and that he had been summoned to Brisbane and the World Genetics Centre for discussions relating to the "Daniel Project".

The flight to Brisbane was scheduled for the following morning, and after Sam had confirmed take-off time with his pilot, the packing of essentials in terms of a change of clothes was completed, with all three looking forward in anticipation to the following day and the flight to the other side of the world.

CHAPTER NINE

The following morning it was a very excited Daniel and Margaret who having had an early breakfast accompanied Sam to Valencia airport where Sam's private X33 was being wheeled out of its hanger as they arrived. Having experienced many flights in the space plane when they visited South America and the Middle East, Daniel's first question was whether as on past occasions he would be able to join the crew of two on the flight-deck. Having had Sam's assurance that this would in all probability the case, all three climbed the gangway and were soon settled in the soft comfortable armchairs of the passenger cabin with its soft lighting and efficient air conditioning.

Prior to take-off, the pilot- James Escorcio who had been Sam's personal pilot for many years, entered the cabin from the flight-deck to welcome them aboard. James was a short swarthy man in his late forties with thick black hair and a neatly trimmed moustache which he kept preening with his fore- finger, a habit that Daniel reckoned was aimed at making sure it was still there. The pleasantries over, James enquired of Daniel whether he wished to observe take-off procedures from the flight-deck and help him plot their flight plan to Brisbane.

As James explained, being a small private plane they had considerable flexibility in planning their flight, with the option of either flying east across the main land masses and then south-east to Australia, or flying west across the Atlantic and Pacific oceans to their destination. After the distances involved and the different time-zones that they would be crossing had been explained and calculated for Daniel's information, he was, much to his delight, given the final say as to which route they would take.

Wanting to view the Andes as he had done on their return flight from South America, Daniel's choice was to fly west, and after a short wait to obtain permission to take-off, they were soon cruising at 45,000 feet over the Atlantic at a speed of sound.

As on previous occasions, Daniel had endless questions to ask James and his co-pilot Antonio - a fair-haired man in his late thirties, who had spent much of his early years as a commercial pilot flying the Atlantic run, and although he had been warned by both Sam and Margaret not to divulge any information that he might have obtained while on the flight-deck of the Anunnaki space ship, his questioning once again caused both pilots to wonder at the intelligence and navigational knowledge of this young boy.

Suddenly the X33 gave a lurch which startled both pilots and sent Daniel who was standing behind the co-pilot's chair, staggering across the cabin. "What was that?" was his immediate reaction. "Don't know", was James response, "but we may have a problem, be a good chap and return to your seat in the passengers' cabin". As Daniel entered he was greeted by a worried Margaret and Sam who had been equally startled by the behaviour of the normally very stable X33.

"James thinks we may have a problem" said Daniel as he strapped himself into his seat. Sam and Margaret exchanged glances but said nothing. A few seconds later a worried sounding James came over the intercom requesting Sam to join him on the flight deck.

Upon entering the flight deck Sam was greeted by two worried faces. We have lost all our navigational equipment James explained and we are now flying blind. "What was our location before they went on the blink?" asked Sam. "We were somewhere over the mid-Atlantic island of Bermuda south of the Atlantic coast of Florida heading for San Juan and Puerto Rico" was Antonio's answer." "That must be fairly close to that area known as Bermuda Triangle" said Sam desperately trying to recall all the legends that he had read about this particular area of the Atlantic Ocean where, over a period of 500 years more than 1,000 incidents of ships and planes having mysteriously vanished without trace, had been recorded. Was there a link between the most unusual behaviour of the X33 and this particular area or was it just a coincidence?

As these thoughts rushed through his mind, the X33 gave another lurch and then appeared to spiral upwards, with both James and Antonio shouting "We've lost control Mr Smith some outside force appears to have taken over control". As they spoke, the cabin lights gradually dimmed and in a few seconds Sam found himself in total darkness as he attempted to return to his beloved Margaret and Daniel.

The next thing that Sam could recall was Daniel's voice calling to him saying "It's alright Uncle Sam, Anu is here with us and we will be OK".

A few minutes later the lights came back on, the door to the passenger cabin was open, and Sam could see Margaret and Daniel in their seats, apparently none the worse for their experience. After giving both a hug Sam turned to Daniel and asked, "Was Anu really here?" "Of course was the boy's response, he is still here and will show himself to you in a few minutes." As he spoke the tall gaunt humanoid figure of Anu materialised, with his long blond hair, deeply tanned skin and startling blue eyes, which as on previous occasions when he had met Daniel, had a hint of warmth and welcome as he stretching out his hands beckoned the boy to come closer, and to touch finger-tips in the traditional greeting.

Sam and Margaret stared fascinated by scene of the old man greeting the young boy, and then by Daniel turning and explaining that Anu welcomed them onboard his star ship, was sorry if the transportation of the X33 into the hold of the ship had given then cause for concern, but could assure them that he wished them no harm, and was delighted at meeting the adopted parents who Daniel had spoken about during his previous visits.

Turning and indicating that he wished them and the two pilots to follow him, Anu opened the door leading from the plane simply by passing his hand over the opening mechanism, and stepped out into the vast hanger-like-hold of the space ship. Anu then proceeded to walk the length of the hold to a lift that carried all five visitors up into the bowels of the ship and eventually to the flight deck described on numerous occasions by Daniel and viewed once by Sam when Daniel was fitted with the visual brain scanner which had recorded what he had seen during his previous teleportation adventures to meet Anu.

Although Margaret had prior knowledge of the existence of Anu and the Anunnaki space ship, the reality of actually being there in the presence of one of the creators of humankind was mind blowing. James and Antonio however, by not having any prior knowledge or idea of these links that Daniel had with the Anunnaki were completely numbed by the whole experience believing that the whole episode was a nightmare from which they would wake up to find themselves still flying the X33 bound for Brisbane Australia.

With Daniel acting as interpreter, Anu went on to explain why he and his colleagues had wanted to meet Daniel's family, the reason being that they had been impressed by the information that the boy had been able to give them of current human society 4,500 years on from their last visit.

They were also aware that Sam had been instrumental in identifying Daniel's unique genome and abilities, and that he had, to a certain extent and on a personal level, achieved through suppression of the aging gene, the long levity which previously had been the sole preserve of the Anunnaki.

Apparently, what they now wanted was further information as to the major developments in human society that had culminated in the establishment of a World Government, and following its establishment its successes and failures.

As Daniel was speaking, Sam vividly recalled the long discussions that he had with Margaret regarding such developments and the research that she had undertaken during Daniel's absence, in the hope that one day they could, on his return, further educate him in major developments of humankind. Little did they know at that time that the information gathered would be crucial to the Anunnaki in their preparation for a return to earth.

CHAPTER TEN

Mark Andrews Director of the World Genetics Centre opened the door of his executive suite on the top floor of the Centre in Brisbane, and after bidding his personal assistant Alice, who was already at her desk, morning greetings, strode across the reception area to his office. As he settled behind his desk and switched on his computer, his personal handset blipped. "A personal call for you sir from the Director of the World Aviation Authority", Alice explained, transferring the call as she spoke. Wondering why that organisation was contacting him at director-level, Mark's response was curt and to the point. "Mark Andrews speaking how can I help you?"

The voice at the other end was strained and apologetic, as if the caller wished the call had not been necessary.

"Dr Andrews this is Rafael Dumas of the W.A.A. speaking, I am sorry to disturb you but we require confirmation and information regarding the passengers on the X33 private flight from Valencia to Brisbane commissioned by a member of your staff, and which departed Valencia at 09.00 hours local time."

"Can I ask the reason for your enquiry" was Mark's first reaction. "Of course Dr Andrews, but can I assume that you are aware of the flight and the passengers involved?"

"Yes, you have my confirmation, and that the passengers were: my Director of Human Genetic Materials Research Unit at Oxford – Dr Sam Smith, his partner Dr Margaret Palma, their adopted son Daniel Da Silva, the pilot James Cowen and co-pilot Antonio Lux. Now can you tell me what it's all about?"

"I'm sorry Dr Andrews, but I must report that the W.A.A. lost all contact of the flight in question at around 10.00 hours today, and there has been no communication with, or sighting of the plane since."

Mark controlling his raising fear paused, and cradling the handset thought what this devastating news might mean, when he next spoke he had regained his normal composure and mindful of the person at the other end, spoke quietly and deliberately.

"Where was the plane when contact was lost?" The reply did nothing to alleviate his fear and concerns. "Approximately south west of Bermuda according to the report that I have, in an area of the Atlantic Ocean commonly referred to as the *Bermuda Triangle*." "We have instigated a sea and air search and I shall personally update you of the ongoing situation."

With that assurance, Rafael Dumas rang off, leaving a visibly shaken Mark deep in thought, as the news of what had happened and its implications sunk in.

His first action was to contact Andrew Shafter and advise him that the proposed meeting with Sam, Margaret and Daniel would, for technical reasons need to be postponed, since at this stage there were so many uncertainties that he did not want the matter known at government-level, and he also wanted time to think and research what was known of the area where the X33 had apparently disappeared.

After making a personal call to Andrew, Mark spent the rest of the morning on the Internet researching what was known of the Bermuda Triangle, while at the same time making sure that he was free to take any updating calls from Rafael Dumas.

The first article of any kind in which the legend of the Triangle appeared, was in newspapers in September 1950, published through Associated Press. Two years later, *Fate* magazine published "Sea Mystery at our Back Door"- a short article by George Sand covering the loss of several planes and ships, including the disappearance of Flight 19, a group of five U.S. Navy Avenger bombers engaged on a training mission.

Sand's article was the first to identify the triangular area of sea where the losses took place, and further details of Flight 19 disappearance was covered in the April 1962 issue of *American Legion* Magazine, and where it was claimed that officials at the Navy board of inquiry stated that the planes "flew off to Mars". This was the first article to connect the supernatural to Flight 19 together with other mysterious disappearances and place in under the umbrella of a new catchy name: *"The Deadly Bermuda Triangle"*.

In 1963 Sands published his book *"Invisible Horizons"* which was to be followed by John Wallace Spencer's book *"Limbo of the Lost"* in 1969; Charles Berlitz's *"The Bermuda Triangle"* in 1974 , and many others, all keeping to some of the same supernatural elements.

Triangle writers it would appear had used a number of supernatural theories to explain the events and disappearances. One explanation pinned the blame on left-over technology from the mythical lost continent of Atlantis which was the location of an ancient civilisation and which psychics have long predicted will one day be found. Other writers have attributed the events to UFO's and alien abductees, while others attribute disappearances in the Triangle to anomalous or unexplained forces.

Although he had heard of the Triangle, Mark was fascinated by the Internet information and decided to continue with his research and learn more about famous but long forgotten incidents involving the Triangle.

In addition to the disappearance of Flight 19 attributed in the Navy's report to "causes or reasons unknown", there was the disappearance of the USS

Cyclops which went missing without a trace with a crew of 309 sometime after March 4, 1918.

In 1948 a Douglas DC-3 disappeared while on a flight from San Juan, Puerto Rico, to Miami. No trace of the aircraft or the 32 people on board was ever found. A sulphur carrying tanker the SS Marine Sulphur Queen with a crew of 39 was last heard of in February 1963 having apparently "sailed into the unknown"; while in 1955 the pleasure yacht the Connemara 1V was found adrift south of Bermuda with no sign of the crew.

Were these long forgotten mysterious incidents with paranormal undertones linked in any way to the apparent disappearance of the X33? Mark Andrew's thoughts were interrupted by the second call from Rafael Dumas.

"I'm sorry to report Dr Andrews, that we have drawn a blank so far. Our air and sea rescue teams are still searching and the one bit of good news is that there has been no sighting of wreckage, and there were no distress calls prior to the disappearance".

Thanking the caller, Mark put down the handset and set about reviewing the situation in terms of the various possibilities.

Although aviation disasters were now relatively rare as compared with the early and mid 21st century, this was in part due to the much reduced volume of air traffic, with the need for business personnel to undertake inter-continental flights much reduced, and the demise of cheap air travel as a consequence of high fuel-oil costs, and scarce renewable energy, prior to the development of the solar and hydrogen cells as a source of energy during the latter part of that century. There had however been much technological progress in the materials used in aircraft, with space-planes such as the X33 benefiting from the technology used in the construction of space stations and of space probes, resulting in the possibility of material and electronic failure being much reduced.

There was however another factor in the situation - a factor only known to himself and Andrew Shafter - namely that there had been on board the X33 a young man with the ability of making contact with extraterrestrial beings. Was his presence and ability connected with, or the cause of, the disappearance?

CHAPTER ELEVEN

After James and Antonio had been escorted off the flight deck to what would be their temporary quarters while on the Anunnaki space ship, Sam, Margaret and Daniel remained in the company of Anu, with Daniel pointing out the various instruments of flight to Sam, while Margaret was fascinated by the various symbols including the dominant "winged disc" that took pride of place among the numerous other picture-hieroglyphs which, in addition to identifying the various instruments, she assumed, represented the origins of language and communication of the Anunnaki.

Although unable to communicate directly with Anu, Sam was most anxious to ascertain how the X33 had been essentially abducted, would the authorities be aware of what had happened, what information did Anu require of him, and would they be returned safely to earth within a short time-scale?

By means of his ESP talents Daniel was able to communicate these concerns and questions to Anu, who proceeded to invite them all to sit at the circle of seats that occupied the central area of the flight deck. After touching fingers in the traditional manner there followed a session of telepathic conversation between Anu and Daniel during which he was able to obtain the following information which he relayed to Sam and Margaret.

In terms of intercepting the X33 during its flight, Anu confirmed that this was as a consequence of the technology and power-source of the space ship homing onto the only remaining Anunnaki power beacon still active on earth, which had escaped destruction due to its being under the sea in an area once forming part of what had been known as *Atlantis* and which had been colonised at about the same time as the Middle East, Africa and South America.

It was this source of power that had made possible the teleportation of the X33 onto the space ship, having first neutralised the navigational instrumentation and power source of the plane.

It also appeared that this abduction was not the first of its kind, with many others having been undertaken in that area over the millennia with the objective of analysing the genetic makeup, abilities, and characteristics, of humans as they evolved. While these had been random in their selection, this instance was the first planned abduction made possible by the advanced information and communicative skills provided by Daniel, through his initial contact with Adapa, and later with Anu.

Anu then proceeded to give Daniel an assurance that while a genetic analysis of both Sam and Margaret would be the objective, no harm would come to either, and the information obtained would be of great value to the Anunnaki.   In terms of the authorities on earth being made aware of the situation, Anu regretted that this information would not be made available, but that they would all be return to earth in due course and would be at liberty of informing those involved of their experiences and of the fact that in the fullness of time the *Gods would return.*

Mindful of the hiatus that his and Daniel's disappearance would be causing at Brisbane and elsewhere, Sam readily agreed to any genetic assessment, and to answering to the best of his ability all questions that Anu might pose, since although through previous abductions some genetic information had been obtained, it would appear that the Anunnaki had been unable to communicate through telepathy with their abductees, and consequently had learnt little of how the intellect, thinking processes, and communicative skills of their creation had developed.

With Daniel as "interpreter" and Sam with over one hundred years experience of life, this was about to change.

Anu's first question related to the human genome in its present form and the developments that had taken place with regard to its enhancement, the elimination of many genetically inherited diseases, the tailoring of individual genomes to occupational interests, and most importantly of all the suppression of those genes responsible for the ageing process.

This was Sam's area of expertise with a recall that went back to the initial discovery by Watson and Crick in the 1960's, the various breakthroughs in genetic research that followed, to the position by 2060 where nearly all constituents of the human genome and their location on the various chromosomes being identified.

The establishment of DNA data bases of populations by most National Governments towards the middle of the 21st century, and that of the world's population by the late 2080's, enabled individuals with no national affiliations, who had escaped the net of national identification data bases and who were in the main responsible for much of world terrorism, to be identified, apprehended, and placed in high security *type one reservations* established as an alternative to prisons and remand centres.

The spread of terrorism and anti-social behaviour which had plagued societies during the early 21st century, and attributed to excessive use of drugs and alcohol in the young, the breakdown of the long established family structure, the equality of the sexes, conflicting ethnic cultures, the demise, and in some instances, the false interpretation of religious teachings, poor or non-existent parenting, and a dumbing-down of education standards, had resulted in the World Government established in the 2080's being required to consider alternative methods of controlling social behaviour and of propagating and improving the genetic profile of humans in general.

The establishment of In-vitro fertilisation (IVF) centres where couples in a stable relationship could donate eggs and sperm and produce an embryo, and In-vitro embryological (IVE) centres where the embryo would be subjected to genetic screening with any required genetic engineering carried out prior to maturity, was aimed at eradicating unfavourable genetic traits and conditions. There then followed the growing-up stages where the young individual would be brought up in a caring and controlled environment until the age of sixteen, with minimal parental involvement.

The final stage of development involved the occupational education and training of the individual which was tailored to his/her genetic makeup and to the needs of society as a whole.

This was a major change from the traditional family upbringing, and although acceptable to the majority of working partners where traditional pregnancy and time off work was not compatible with their life-style, there was a minority who were unable to accept the concept, choosing to opt out of main stream society and living on *type two reservations* where, although there was a restriction of one child per couple, they were able to bring up their child within the traditional family environment. With their health and screening clinics, research at these reservations provided a rich source of genetic material outside main stream society, and it was in *reservation 229* that Daniel and his unique genome had been discovered.

Alongside these changes had been the need to address the problems that had arisen as a consequence of National governments in the early and mid 21st century promoting multiculturalism and economic migration, which although initially successful had eventually led to racial tensions feed by some irresponsible religious teaching. The advent of multiculturalism was a direct consequence of cheap transport and a global economy driven by global money markets and where another human trait of *greed* played a major part. While it had been recognised by some that such developments were contrary to the initial geographical separation of identifiable ethnic groups as initially introduced by the Anunnaki in their attempt to suppress the inherent tribal and warring attitudes of early human societies, little could be done by National Governments to curtail such economic migration and it was not until the advent of a World Government that alternatives could be considered.

Anu appeared well pleased with this information that Daniel had relayed to him and suggested that they have a break, continuing some time later.

CHAPTER TWELVE

As the questioning proceeded, Sam was thankful for the research that Margaret had undertaken during the period of Daniel's disappearance, in identifying what she considered had been the major factors contributing to world society in 2112, since without such advanced knowledge, he felt sure that he would have encountered considerable difficulty in responding to Anu's questions.

In addition to seeking information as to what had occurred in human society in recent times, Anu was anxious to ascertain what, in Sam's opinion, were the reasons behind such occurrences. This task he considered a daunting one, but again thanks to the numerous debates with Margaret, he felt reasonably competent to respond to most, especially as Margaret was sitting by his side, and although not responding directly, gave him the occasional nudge or prompt by a squeeze of the hand or a glance of approval.

As Sam recalled, the major developments that had occurred during the late 20th and the first half of the 21st century were: the emergence of the Global Economy with Multinational Companies having the power to switch their activities world wide for purely economic and profit making reasons, with no reference to any National Government; the establishment of a poorly regulated Global Money Market which was open to corruption, yet with the power to destabilise national currencies, businesses, and the whole economy of countries. Coupled with the establishment of a Global Economy was the ever increasing power and influence of the World Media and the unregulated Information Highway.

The combined effects of these developments over a period of time had resulted in elected National

Governments loosing their ability to govern, with politicians making promises that they had little or no chance of keeping. This in turn had resulted in a sharp decline in political awareness and interest, with politicians world-wide being regarded as false, greedy and unworthy of the peoples' trust.

The onset of what could be described as Economic Terrorism with money and share markets being manipulated by unscrupulous individuals marked the final chapter in the survival of National Governments, with the emergence of a World Government run by highly educated and experienced men and women with no political affiliations or ambitions, and with a engineered genome where the aging gene combination had been suppressed allowing for long levity, being at the time, the only viable option.

The establishment of World Government and a single currency immediately removed the influence of rogue traders on money markets and currency trading, as well as removing and price differential between global regions. This made possible the establishment of five Regional Trading Areas (ATA'S) aimed at servicing the populations of the five geographical regions, that although initially self governing, through amalgamation in 2085, were now the power blocks of World Government.

This equalisation of business, commerce and service industries across the globe, removed the need for economic migration, and made easer the repatriation of ethnic communities to their homelands, and essentially reversing the trend towards multi-culture societies.

Another beneficial side-effect of such regional economies, was a major reduction in the global trafficking of foods and consumables, with the need to transport consumables half-way round the world and from continent to continent removed, with a consequent reduction in the unit cost of products due to there being a massive saving on transport costs.

This reduction was also contributory to a reduction in fossil fuel consumption which peaked with the advent of the solar and hydrogen cell as a source of alternative energy, while the nuclear power stations and wind-farms of the 20th and 21st century were systematically decommissioned.

The development of the hydrogen cell in all its various forms made public transport very inexpensive, and coupled to a mono-rail infrastructure which linked centres of population, diminished the need for personal transport in towns and cities. Personal transport in the form of a hydrogen cell powered vehicle became the preserve of government executives and the like with traffic pollution practically nonexistent.

This alternative source of energy also provided the human race with the power necessary to escape the Earth's gravitational pull and enter space, thus conquering what to mankind had been the *final frontier*.

Although the development of space flight had its roots in the latter part of the 20th century with strong competition between America and Russia, with America winning the race to land the first astronauts on the moon, continuing development by an European consortium and by China, were hampered by the ever present problem of the power to size ratio, and although the American *Shuttle* space craft was partly successful in overcoming this problem, it was not until the advent of the hydrogen cell in the latter part of the 21st century, that the building of orbiting space stations, space telescopes, and the sending of scientific probes into outer space had possible.

At the level of the individual, all forms of credit were subject to strict regulation, with those possessing credit cards being subject to automatic limits which were directly related to earnings. Credit facilities were not being available in either type of *reservation*. Earnings were also set within established bands, as were all forms of taxation. Bonus payments which had been the feature of the early and mid 21st century were made illegal with both business and the individual prosecuted should such activity occur.

As the levels of borrowing dramatically declined, there had been major shift in   business practice, with the profit-ethos of the late 20th and early 21st centuries being replaced by a more service-centered economy.

Although still existing in *Type one reservations,* the decline in all forms of religious teachings had been a significant feature of main-stream 21st century society, with churches, chapels, mosques, and other centres for worship experiencing a dramatic decline in attendance.

At this point Anu raised his hand and Daniel whispered to Sam, "You can stop now Uncle Sam, Anu has heard enough, is very happy with what you have told him, and believes that mankind is well on the road to establishing the kind of civilisation that 450,000 years ago was the Anunnaki dream."

Although he was not aware at the time, Sam now felt completely drained by the experience of answering, via Daniel, all Anu's questions, and was relieved that a halt had been called. Daniel was apparently unaffected by the whole process and continued to converse with Anu by their special form of ESP, as he moved around the flight deck checking then various instruments and dials.

Returning to where Sam and Margaret were sitting Daniel said "Anu now wishes that you take a rest in your quarters that he has prepared for you, and after that he would appreciate your and Aunty Margaret's co-operation in the genetic screening programme which he believes will indicate further, the progress made in the evolution of mankind."

CHAPTER THIRTEEN

Mark Andrews' executive suite was silent but for the soft hum of conversation emanating from the five seated round the large highly polished plate-glass committee table that occupied one side of his office. At the head of the table was Andrew Shafter accompanied by his personal assistant, across the table was Rafael Dumas, who had been summoned from the WAA Centre in Huston to appear in person, while opposite him was Mark accompanied by his assistant. It was after much deliberation that Mark had concluded that Andrew Shafter must be informed of the disappearance of the X33 and its passengers while on route to Brisbane, and that Rafael Dumas must be made aware of who the passengers were, and of the probable consequences of such an unexplained disappearance.

Ten hours had elapsed since Rafael had made his first contact with Mark advising him of the X33's disappearance, and six hours had elapsed since he was contacted by the World Transport Minister instructing him to fly immediately to Brisbane and report in person to Mark Andrews and Andrew Shafter.

Following the customary introductions, discussions had commenced by Rafael reiterating the events of the last ten hours. He noted the sudden and inexplicable disappearance of the X33 from the WAA radar, the failure of the WAA to make any subsequent contact with the flight, and the failure by the air and sea search that followed the reported disappearance, to locate any wreckage had the plane crashed. He was then question as to other possibilities, but other than the pilot deliberating flying off into space, or the complete failure of the plane's automatic navigation system, resulting in a similar possibility, he had no suggestions

Since it was obvious that Rafael was intrigued by the level of interest at Ministerial level that this disappearance had generated, Andrew Shafter had concluded that he should be given outline details of the situation and of the fact that the X33 was carrying a young man with extraordinary psychokinetic, telekinetic and psychoportation abilities, and with the ability of communicating with the extraterrestrial Anunnaki. When he had finished it was a shocked and almost unbelieving Rafael Dumas who gazing round the table muttered, "I will do everything possible to ensure that the current search is comprehensive and that it will continue until we have a result- be it good or bad." At which point his mobile implant began to vibrate and reaching for his handset he contacted his office in Huston to receive another update that again recorded no sightings or information in relation to the X33 flight.

Following a further few minutes conversation the meeting broke up with Rafael returning to Brisbane airport for his return private flight to Huston, and Andrew Shafter returning to the World Government offices in Beijing to report on the situation which to-date had been restricted to his own department.

Back on board the Anunnaki space ship Sam and Margaret woke refreshed from a sleep that they never thought they would enjoy. Their accommodation although spartan was comfortable, with Daniel who had escorted then to the cabin assuring them that everything would be alright and that they would come to no harm. Then the events of the immediate past came flooding back, and unreal as it might seem, they both realised that it had not been a dream and they really were on an Anunnaki space ship some where in space.

At that point Daniel entered the cabin to inform them that he had visited James and Antonio and that they were fine although confused by past events, and that Anu wished to see them prior to the body screening which he was anxious to undertake. With Daniel leading, Sam and Margaret were led to another part of the ship that resembled a laboratory of sorts and where Anu greeted them in his usual courteous but silent manner. Although this silence Sam found rather disturbing, and while he was very much aware that communication in the world language of English was not possible, he had the feeling that Anu could read his thoughts and in some way was aware of what he was going to say to Daniel before he actually said it.

The screening appeared to take the form of the well established total- body scan used in hospitals throughout the world, with both Sam and Margaret while in the prone position being passed through a scanning tunnel – a procedure that took around ten minutes by Sam's calculation, appeared to be all embracing with genetical, mental, anatomical, and physical properties being recorded simultaneously. Following completion of the screening procedure, Daniel escorted them back to their quarters, where they spent the next few hours asking all the questions that had built up in both their minds since the initial abduction. Such questions as what would happen next, would James and Antonio be screened, when would they be able to leave and return to earth, and was there any possibility of letting Brisbane know that they were all safe?

Although Daniel was unable to say what would happen next or when they would be leaving, he was able to say that from his very first meeting with Anu, it had been made clear to him that what the Anunnaki wished for was to establish a picture of what human society was like in 2112, identify any significant changes in the human genome as a consequence of random selection or genetic engineering, and to consider whether those major developments, both scientific and other, that had taken place over the last 4,500 years were attributable to individuals who, possibly through this random combination of genetic material, had inherited some qualities previously only attributable to their creators.

As Daniel recalled, one of the many questions asked him during his initial meeting with Anu was whether he could identify those humans whose knowledge, skills, and desire to learn, had significantly contributed to and changed human society in general. In this context he had relied on the teachings of Margaret, his visiting tutors and Professor Regina Poveda who had been instrumental in developing his artistic skills.

Among those that he had listed were the leaders of the early Sumerian and Mayan civilisations, the Egyptian pharaohs, the Inca emperors, Greeks such as Aristotle and Plato, Romans such as Michael Angelo and Leonardo da Vinci, Jesus of Nazareth the founder of Christianity, European scientists such as Einstein, Isaac Newton, Marconi, Watson and Crick, and numerous others whose inventions had changed human understanding of what was possible.

Also included were those leaders who through their ethnic background, religious beliefs, greed and the desire for power and domination, had wedged wars against their neighbours, and again, in some instances, changed the face of society and the world in general.

In terms of the suggestion that he make contact with someone on earth, in a similar way to his initial contact with Adapa, Daniel was unsure but as he promised Margaret and Sam, he was prepared to try although he had no knowledge of whether it was achievable without his teleportation back to earth, probably against the wishes of Anu.

CHAPTER FOURTEEN

Professor Regina Poveda woke with a start from what for her was an unusually disturbed sleep. As the familiar objects of her bedroom came into focus in the dawn light that was breaking over the orange groves of Monte Picio situated some twenty kilometres outside Valencia, she recalled vividly the dream in which the young man Daniel Da Silva, who she had tutored around two years previously, had entered her bedroom, placed something on her bedside table, smiled down at her and then disappeared. The incident had appeared so real that only her waking made her realise that it had in effect only been a dream.

Regina Poveda was, even at the age of sixty seven years, a strikingly beautiful woman, with dark brown eyes, flawless tanned skin, a figure worthy of a woman forty years her junior, with the only indication of aging being the streaks of grey in her dark brown hair that she normally wore in a bun at the nap of her neck, but was now spread across the pillows of the large double bed which she had always slept in since making the house her home some thirty years previous. Of Spanish/Portuguese origin, her appearance and life style was in many ways a throw-back to the traditional Spanish lady of the early 20th century, an image enhanced by the fact that her home was an old traditional Spanish country house built almost three centuries previous and situated amongst the orange groves of Monte Picio.

Although during her lifetime she had many lovers, she had never married or been in a long-term relationship, and her current family consisted of an elderly married couple who saw to her domestic needs, ran the household, and ensured that her lifestyle was comparable to a lady of her social standing and wealth.

Prior to her retirement at the age of sixty she had lectured part-time at Valencia's University while also being the Director of the Valencia Museum of Arts, and following her retirement she had been installed as Emeritus Professor at the University.

Lying in bed watching the first rays of the morning sun streaming through the partly drawn curtains, she vividly recalled her first encounter with Daniel and how she had taken an immediate liking to the young man with his curly black hair, large brown eyes fringed with those long eye lashes that any woman would die for.

That he possessed an intellect way beyond his years and extraordinary talents that she was to discover later, all added up to her always recalling their time together with pleasure and pride, but with much sadness when he suddenly stopped attending the tutorials and practical classes that they both enjoyed so much, apparently leaving Valencia to stay with relatives in his home region of New Mexico.

She also recalled the various discussions they had during his weekly visits to Monte Picio, and Daniel's unbelievable explanations of the oil painting and water colour that he had completed as part of his studies, and where he had exhibited artistic talents that, in Regina's opinion, equalled those of Michael Angelo, Leonardo Da Vinci and other great artists of the past. In particular, she remembered the oil painting depicting an old man with dark aquiline features, piercing deeply set dark eyes, white flowing hair and beard, wearing a long white robe against a background of lush green jungle-like vegetation, which Daniel had identified as Adapa - a guide of the Anunnaki.

A gentle tap on the bedroom door brought her back to the present, with Lugia her maid bustling in with her morning cup of coffee which she always enjoyed prior to going downstairs for her very traditional Spanish breakfast of Serrano ham, home-baked bread and fruit. As Lugia drew back the curtains and the morning sunlight streamed into the bedroom, Regina noticed for the first time the small scrap of paper that lay on her bedside table. Stretching over she picked it up and gave a gasp of astonishment, for written in the script-like hand writing which she immediately recognised, was the following message.

Dear Professor Poveda, Uncle Sam, Aunty Margaret and I are currently with the Anunnaki on board one of their space ships, please contact Dr Mark Andrews at the World Genetics Centre in Brisbane to let him know that we are all OK. Kindest regards, Daniel Da Silva.

Sitting up in bed Regina stared at the neatly written note, recalling her dream of Daniel being in her bedroom and now wondering if it had indeed been a dream. Had Daniel using his teleportation skills visited her bedroom, or had he through his telekinetic skills caused the note to appear on her bedside table?
His message giving his location on board a space ship, and the request that she contact someone in an organisation she had no knowledge of, advising him of his safety was equally unbelievable.

Her thoughts were interrupted by Lugia enquiring "Are you all right madam?" to which   Regina's response was "Yes, I'm alright just had a very peculiar dream." At which point Lugia left the room leaving Regina with her thoughts and how was she going to respond to Daniel's request.

As she recalled the world internet of the early and mid 21st century, had upon the establishment of World Government, been drastically modified. This move had been initiated in order to remove the unacceptable levels of misinformation and ignorance that existed on the web, and which had created generations of "digitally addicted" users who, in addition to precipitating unacceptable levels of inattention and stupidity, had eroded moral boundaries to a point where the individual's sense of what was true and what was false and what was real and what was imaginary, had been significantly affected.

Another effect of these changes was to restrict the vast majority of web users to their particular geographical web providers, with world-wide access across the five regions restricted to government officials and the like. Mobile handsets however were not subject to such restriction in terms of normal conversation provided the caller had access to that particular number.

Having showered, dressed and eaten her usual breakfast of orange juice toast and black coffee, Regina's first task consequently, was to ascertain the number of the World Genetic Centre in Brisbane. Through her regional web provider she soon located the number of the European Regional Genetic Materials Research Unit in Oxford, which from her recollection of a conversation with Sam, was were he worked as Director.

Noting the name and access number of the new Director - Edward Chapman, she proceeded to dial the number. An automated answering service eventually located the director's office and she put her request to his personal assistant, who, after verification as to who was calling and the nature of her business with Brisbane, gave her a number which she could use.

Regina waited as the automated answering service at the World Genetics Centre churned out the various options, which eventually resulted in her speaking to Mark Andrew's personal assistant. Again the process of verification had to be dealt with, with Regina insisting that she must speak to Mark Andrews in person, and on a highly confidential matter. After a few minutes the handset came to life with a voice saying -"Mark Andrews here, how can I help?"

CHAPTER FIFTEEN

Mark Andrew's phone bleeped and his personal assistant informed him that she had a call from an unknown source wishing to speak with him on a highly confidential matter regarding Daniel Da Silva, with the lady caller refusing to give any information other than to the director. Since the last twenty four hours had seen Mark desperately waiting for news from the WAA, with Raphael Dumas although ringing at two hourly intervals, unable to provide any information as to the whereabouts or fate of the X33, the possibility of information from some other source had not crossed his mind until now.

"Mark Andrews here, how can I help you?" The highly cultured voice that spoke English with a hint of a Southern European dialect, spoke quickly and clearly.

"Dr Andrews, my name is Regina Poveda at one time a private tutor to a young man - Daniel Da Silva, he has contacted me and requested that I inform you that he and his Uncle and Aunt are safe and well and are on board a space ship of the Anunnaki."

Although normally calm and unruffled, this astonishing news from a source that he had scant knowledge of, apart from a recollection that in one of Sam's numerous reports it had been mentioned that Daniel had a tutor in the Arts, who was a retired professor and who was immensely impressed by his talents, rendered Mark speechless for a few seconds, while his brain raced for a possible explanation.

Quickly gathering his thoughts and ever mindful of the need for security he continued the conversation having ensured that the recording facility was in place.

"Professor Poveda, thank you for this information which I very much hope that you will appreciate will require verification in terms of your identity, how were you able to contact me, and how you became privy to this information, which I trust you will realise will be classified and subject to the strictest security".

Regina's response was brief and succinct, "Dr Andrews, since you appear to be aware of my professional background, I can only suggest that in order to verify where I live, and how I came into possession of this information, you had better visit me at my home in Monte Picio, where you will be most welcome. I have always had a great deal of time for Daniel, and in the short time I knew him became very fond of him both as a person and as someone with extraordinary artistic talents which I believe you are aware of, and may have actually viewed. I am aware of the need for the utmost security, since I was security-screened prior to becoming his tutor, and can assure you that I will comply in every way possible if it means his continued safety and well-being and eventual return to earth."

At this point in the conversation Mark assured her of his understanding of the situation from her point of view, and on impulse, informed her that he would by flying to Valencia immediately with a view to discussing the issues further since it was obvious that for some unknown reason, she had apparently been selected by Daniel to be the point of contact and the means by which he could relay information back to earth.

Having instructed his personal assistant to contact his private plane to request the pilot to make the necessary arrangements for an immediate flight to Valencia, Mark contacted Andrew Shafter advising him of the fact that it would appear that Daniel had made contact with his erstwhile tutor advising her that the X33 had been abducted by the Anunnaki, that all on board were fit and well, and that he would be travelling to Valencia to meet Professor Poveda to verify the details within the next few hours.

He then contacted Rafael Dumas advising him to discontinue the search for the X33, emphasising that under the official secrets Act he was not at liberty to divulge the reason for such action, but that it would in no way affect the reputation or perceived competence of the World Aviation Authority.

As Mark was about to leave for the airport, he received an e-mail from Edward Chapman requesting information relating to Sam's visit to Brisbane, and whether any decisions taken would affect his position of Acting Director at Oxford. In concluding the e-mail, he reported that a request for information relating to Mark's contact number had been made by source apparently known to Sam, and although this information had been given, it had not been authorised by him, and that he was contemplating disciplinary action against the member of staff involved.

Mindful of the fact that Edward had always resented the fact that on the onset of Sam's sabbatical leave to continue his studies of Daniel's genome, he had only been appointed as acting director and not given the status that came with the permanent post, and that he still resented the fact that he had not been made privy to Sam's discovery of Daniel's unique talents, Mark decided not to respond to the mail, leaving his office for the airport and his flight to Valencia.

Relaxing in the artificially lit four-seat cabin of the X33 as it powered out of Brisbane airport, Mark recalled his conversation with Regina Poveda and the almost unbelievable news of the abduction of an X33 complete with pilots and passengers by extra terrestrials- the Anunnaki. He also recalled the various reports that Sam had submitted since first making contact with Daniel. The discovery of his unique genome linked to hitherto undiscovered brain activity. The recorded, and scientifically verified, evidence of his unique telekinetic, teleportation and ESP abilities, culminating in the "Princeton" experiment and the recording of his meeting Anu on board the Anunnaki space ship.

Although these discoveries relating to Daniel unique abilities had been considered seriously by Mark and Andrew Shafter, Mark had tended to mentally isolate the findings from his main stream thinking. The disappearance of the X33 together with its crew and passengers however, brought home to him the potential enormity of the situation should the world at large became aware of the existence of an extraterrestrial humanoid race - the Anunnaki, who in their role as creators of the human race intended to return to earth after an intervening period of around 4,500 years.

CHAPTER SIXTEEN

Upon arrival at Valencia's airport where he was met by the driver of the personal transport that had been arranged for him, Mark was soon heading north towards the orange groves of Monte Picio. Being a local resident the driver was familiar with the roads and very soon was turning into the tree-lined driveway that led to the traditional Spanish-style villa which was the home of Professor Regina Poveda.

Having made contact on arrival at Valencia airport and having advised her of his estimated time of arrival, Mark was greeted by a smiling Regina Poveda who warmly welcomed him to Valencia and to her home.

Upon entering her elegant living area with its wealth of oil paintings and artefacts of a long past Spanish culture, all very much in keeping with her past position as Director of the Museum of Art at Valencia, and Professor of Art at the University, Mark was served the traditional coffee by Lugia who together with her partner Manuel ran the household.

After the conventional pleasantries including an enquiry as to whether his journey had been comfortable Regina handed Mark the note she had discovered on her bedside table the previous morning.

In the silence that followed Mark studied the brief message written in the script-like hand writing of a young person which confirmed what Regina had told him over the qPhone.

Dear Professor Poveda, Uncle Sam, Aunty Margaret and I are currently with the Anunnaki on board one of their space ships, please contact Dr Mark Andrews at the World Genetics Centre in Brisbane to let him know that we are all OK. Kindest regards, Daniel Da Silva.

Turning to Regina, Mark asked "How do you think this note came to be on your bedside table, and did you know prior to the note that Daniel and his adopted parents were missing?"

Regina's response was quick and precise- "In answer to the last part of your question I had no idea that anything untoward had happened to Daniel and his family since I have had no contact with them for months." "How the message came to be on my bedside table I have no idea, other than the fact that I did have a very vivid dream where Daniel entered my bedroom, placed something on the table, smiled down at me and then disappeared." "On reflection, I have been wondering if in fact this was a dream in the normal sense, or was it Daniel making contact through his undoubted extra-sensory abilities."

Mark pondered on what she had said while again reading Daniel's message. "Why do you think he contacted you?!" was Mark's next question. "I have no idea except that during the time he was my pupil, I always felt that he knew what question I was about to ask before I actually asked it, and always gave the answer word for word as I would have given it myself."

Being very aware of all that Sam and told him about Daniel, Mark could appreciate Regina's observations and let the matter drop.

"Is there anything more that I can do?" asked Regina. Choosing his words carefully Mark responded - "For the time being, I cannot see anything that you or I can do except wait and hope that Daniel's assurance that everyone is safe and sound is correct. In the meantime it is essential that this development is kept secret, as indeed is the whole situation, since the total disappearance of a Government commissioned space plane with all its passengers and crew would cause worldwide public concern."

"Do you think that this abduction is a prelude to further developments involving the Anunnaki?" was Regina's next question.

Although Mark had tended to place this possibility to the back of his mind, the question raised by someone who had little or no knowledge of any such possibility, made him realise that the problems that he faced were no longer just his to be considered and dealt with under the stewardship of Andrew Shafter and the World Population Trends and Development committee, but would be relevant to all human beings.

"I do not know" was Mark's eventual response, "But all the indications given by Daniel are that that the planet Nibiru which we are given to understand is, or was once, the home of the Anunnaki, will be at its nearest point to Earth sometime during the year 2112, and we are already some way through that year, and should the Anunnaki intend to visit the Earth once again, this most certainly would be the time."

At this point in the discussion, Lugia announced that the meal that Regina had requested her to prepare was ready for serving. Regina escorted Mark into the adjoining dinning room where, over the excellent prepared Valencian paella washed down with some of Regina's best Rioja, they were soon engaged in discussions relating to their careers and the changes that both had experienced since the disappearance of the Nation-State and the establishment of a World Government. Both agreed that the changes had been due primarily to individual countries inability to function independently within the Global economy, coupled with the credibility of the professional politician being eroded to such an extent that they no longer had the trust of the people, that establishment of World Government made up of knowledgeable, intelligent and influential men and women, was the only alternative.

In Regina's opinion these changes had also been brought about as a consequence of numerous other factors including - ethnic-based world wide terrorism, aggressive media advertising, the greed of individuals and societies, uncontrolled lending of money with little chance of repayment, uncontrolled internet pornography, uncontrolled international commerce with profit-making as its primary objective, human excesses and intolerance, the dumbing down of long established education systems, the failure of the family as a social unit, poor or non-existent parenting, and uncontrolled economic migration.

What had been the benefits of these changes? Both were in agreement that the establishment of Reservations had been a good thing in as much as Type one reservations removed the antiquated prison and detention systems, allowing the convicted controlled freedom and work opportunities within strict parameters, while Type two reservations enabled those wishing to opt-out of main-stream society to do so, and continue their chosen way of life, be it within controlled limits.

These developments had only been made possible through the establishment of World Government, DNA profiling of main-stream society, the repatriation of ethnic minorities to their areas of origin, the enhancement of the human genome through genetic engineering with the removal or suppression of many genetically inherited conditions, and above all the suppression of the ageing gene.

As they rounded off the meal with coffee and a glass of Regina's excellent cognac, both were in agreement that their perceptions of the development of the world over the last decades were very much in line, while it appeared that they might, through pure chance, have a role to play in the future of world development through a link with a young man called Daniel.

CHAPTER SEVENTEEN

Sam woke from a troubled sleep to find Daniel standing by the side of his bunk which was of the pull-down type fixed to the wall of the windowless cabin of the Anunnaki space ship. Margaret occupied a similar structure to his left, and now stirred restlessly in her sleep.

"Is everything alright?" Sam asked as he blinked the sleep out of his eyes and focused on boy.

"Anu has told me that we can leave and return to Earth, since he believes he has all the information that we can give him about the world of 2112."

Sam shot up in his bunk, and threw his arms round Daniel, hugging him and shouting, "Margaret, wake up we have great news." Struggling to sit upright in her bunk, Margaret stared at Daniel and Sam and in a sleepy voice demanded to know what the problem was. "Daniel tells me that Anu is ready for us to return to Earth, and that as a result of what we have told him and the genetic screening that we underwent, he has all the information that he could reasonably have expected of us."

With Daniel leading, they made their way to the accommodation shared by James and his co-pilot Antonio, and having told them the good news, made their way to the fight deck, where Anu greeted them in his customary fashion. With Daniel again acting as interpreter in translating Anu's thoughts into words, they were told that their stay on board the space vessel was over and that soon the X33 with its passengers and crew would be returned to the exact location from where they were initially abducted.

Anu wished to thank them for their co-operation in providing invaluable information about current World Government and society in general, and for the genetic information resulting from their screening, which he and the Anunnaki considered vital to their preparation for a return visit to Earth after an interval of 4,500 earth years, and 450,000 earth years since their first visitation. At this point, Sam was unable to contain himself and stage-whispered to Daniel "Ask him when they are coming and where will they be landing?"

While Daniel communicated the request to Anu, Margaret squeezed Sam's hand and whispered, "Don't ask any more questions, just in case you upset him." Sam gave her hand a reassuring squeeze as Daniel turned away from Anu and said.

"Anu informs me that the visitation will follow the same pattern as that of previous visits by his ancestors which have occurred at regular intervals over a period of 450,000 earth years. They will use the pyramids of South America and Egypt as "markers" and then use the Earth's ley lines and their intersection for a more detailed guidance as to where they wish to land. He gave me more details but we don't have the time right now for me to explain fully, but I will once we are back on the X33."

At which point Anu raised his hands as a sign of farewell, and with Daniel in the lead all five made their way to the vast cargo-hold of the space ship where the X33 stood exactly as they had left it. Although there appeared to be no sign of any other vehicles in the hold, Sam was quite sure that there would have been enough room to dock several space vehicles, should the need arise. Upon entering the X33, James turned to Sam and enquired "What do we do now and how do we get out of here?"

Before Sam could respond, Daniel spoke up saying, "It's OK James, just carry out your normal pre take-off procedures and Anu will do the rest, by teleporting the X33 to its original flight path and location."

Looking rather stunned by this news, James and Antonio entered the flight deck and proceeded to carry out the systematic pre take-off procedures, watched by Daniel, while Sam and Margaret settled down in their seats in the passenger cabin to await take-off.

One minute they were in the cargo hold of the Anunnaki space ship and the next the X33 with all its navigational instrumentation working, was flying westwards over the Atlantic Ocean heading for San Juan and Puerto Rico. James and Antonio gave a whoop of joy, and turning to Daniel who was still standing behind James' chair, both extended their hands saying "Well done man you were right and we are now OK, thanks to you."

With his co-pilot left to plot their flight path to Brisbane, James accompanied by Daniel returned to the passenger cabin to discuss with Sam what information should be transmitted to Brisbane and to the WAA, since he was very aware that the latter would by now have recorded the reappearance of the X33 on their radar screens, and would immediately launch an enquiry into the circumstances surrounding its initial disappearance and now its return. Sam was also very aware of the potential problems in accounting for these events and immediately instructed James to ensure that he used the high security communication link, restrict the amount of information to the minimum only advising the WAA that their technical problems had been resolved, and of their estimated time of arrival at Brisbane. A similar message should also be sent to Mark Andrews at the World Genetics Centre.

As James returned to the flight deck and Daniel settled down in his seat, Margaret reminded him of his promise to give them more details of what Anu had told him about the Anunnaki's impending return to Earth. Did he indicate when, why and where, were the questions that sprang to her lips. Choosing his words carefully, Daniel proceeded to explain to Margaret and Sam the essentials of what Anu had told to him.

Apparently the most important aspect of the impending visit related to the same reason as to why the Anunnaki had made repeated visits to Earth over the last 450,000 years. This was to monitor the progress that their creation had made during the intervening period, and the evolutionary development made by humans towards the goals and expectations initially programmed into the human genome.

In this context Anu had made it clear to Daniel that during their various visits the Anunnaki had not been pleased with what they discovered with regard to the characteristics, trends and behaviour of their creation, and in some instances had taken draconian action to remedy some of the problems that they had discovered.

At the root of these various problems was the continued tribal and clan mentality that humans had inherited from their original primate ancestors and which the Anunnaki had failed to remove during the initial engineering of the human genome. This, together with greed and the desire to dominate that occurred between communities had, in some instances necessitated the annihilation of whole tribes and communities. An example of such retribution had been recorded in the Bible with the destruction of Sodom and Gomorra. The initial geographical separation and labelling of these various fractions had initially reduced tribal conflict, but as humans developed the means of migration and travel over long distances and from one geographical region to another, mainly as a consequence of the development of the boat as a means of travel over water, conflict returned, with tribal wars and invasions.

84

The occasional emergence of individuals with exceptional abilities and talents akin to those embedded initially in the human genome, but blocked for safety reasons, and which had emerged as a consequence of a random combination of genetic material, had also been an aspect of monitoring by the Anunnaki through the "messengers" such as Adapa who, while remaining on Earth, reported such occurrences.

It was these individuals that had contributed greatly to the development of the species as a whole.

In relation to the exact timing and location of their arrival on Earth, Anu had been more guarded in the information he passed on to Daniel, only indicating that it would be sometime during the Earth year of 2112, and at a location that had been used by the Anunnaki on various other occasions.

As Daniel completed his account, James entered the cabin to announce that they would be arriving at Brisbane in a few minutes.

CHAPTER EIGHTEEN

Mark Andrews had just stepped off his return flight from Valencia, when he received the message on his qphone that informed him that, following technical problems the X33 with Sam, Margaret, and Daniel on board, would be landing at Brisbane within the hour.

Arriving at his office Mark's first thought was to contact Regina Poveda in Valencia to inform her of the wonderful news, since in the short time he had spent with her he had come to realise that this highly intelligent woman had developed strong feelings towards Daniel, and had been genuinely concerned at his disappearance but equally thankful that by some teleportation process he had been able to contact her to let her know that they were all safe in the presence of the Anunnaki. His message by a qphone text simply said "Daniel is back". He then proceeded to contact Andrew Shafter with a similar message, while at the same time contacting Raphael Dumas to confirm that the WAA had located and were monitoring the X33's flight to Brisbane.

As he sat behind his desk awaiting their arrival, Mark's thoughts were racing as he considered the possibilities of what their experiences over the last forty eight hours had been, where they had been, who they had met, and what they had learnt. Aircraft and ships had disappeared before, as had individuals, but until now, none had returned to tell their story, if a story was there to be told.

Mark also considered what the consequences of the disappearance and return of the X33 and its passengers would have been had it occurred during the late 20th and early 21st century when media coverage of such events had reached unacceptable levels of intrusion and speculation, with reporting bearing little or no relationship to the factual situation.

This situation had eventually led to the strict control of world media reporting and the gradual demise of both national and commercial media to be replaced by a World Government News Network reporting facts as opposed to the previous mix of speculation, opinions, and distorted facts. Mark's thoughts were interrupted by his personal assistant entering the office to advise him that his guests had arrived.

As Sam, Margaret and Daniel entered the office they were greeted by a relieved Mark, who expressed his delight at their safe arrival and on meeting Daniel for the first time. Daniel in his usual old-fashioned manner greeted Mark with a shake of the hand and a slight bow of the head, announcing that he was pleased that he had at last met Uncle Sam's boss.

After Mark had got them seated and served with coffee with Daniel choosing a fruit juice, his pent-up curiosity got the better of him, and turning to Sam said, "Now tell me where have you been, who did you meet, and what did you discover?"

Over the next hour or so Sam, with the occasional prompt from Margaret and Daniel, recalled the events that had began with the teleportation of the X33 from its flight path over the West Atlantic to the Anunnaki space ship, and ended with the X33 being teleported back to its original point of abduction some forty eight hours later.

Mark sat enthralled as Sam described their first meeting with Anu, and how, although he had an idea from Daniel's account of similar meetings, and had seen Anu through Daniel's brain-scan recording and the painting of Anu that he had completed for Professor Poveda, their meeting face to face had been very different, and had brought with it the realisation that they were in the presence of a being who could well have been described as a *God* by ancient cultures.

When he had finished Mark turned to Daniel and said, "Well young man since you were the communication "link" between Anu and your uncle, was his description of what happened correct, did he miss out anything and do you want to add anything further?"

After giving the question some thought, Daniel, in his usual precise manner, proceeded by saying that throughout his numerous meetings and ESP communication with, firstly with Adapa, and then with Anu, he had been made very aware that the information that the Anunnaki sought as a precursor to their return visit to Earth was aimed not only at monitoring the progress made by humans, but at promoting the best interests of the species that they had created some 450,000 years previously.

It had also been clear from what Adapa and Anu had indicated, that on previous visits the Anunnaki had been disappointed with the progress and activities of their creation, and the fact that despite their initial teachings, humans had in the main tended to replicate what they could recall through a fading genetic memory, of the activities of the *Gods,* while at the same time still exhibiting the aggressive and territorial instincts of their *primate* ancestors, which had in some instances had required drastic action in an attempt to eliminate some of the most unfavourable of traits.

Mindful of the undoubted power of the Anunnaki such measures had included the annihilation of whole communities, with some such events appearing in early recorded history.

He also viewed the information that Sam and Margaret had been able to pass on to Anu as being most welcomed, since the changes that had taken place since the last visit by the Anunnaki, which was approximately 2,500 years before the birth of Jesus Christ, had been on an unbelievable scale, due in the main to a massive improvement in human intelligence with some individuals, apparently at random, exhibiting outstanding talents and inventive skills, that had catapulted human knowledge and development forward in a way that tended to replicate the talents of its creators.

In the areas of science such as genetic engineering, where Sam had been able to provide details of the progress made, to space exploration and the discovery of the planet Nibiru towards the end of the 21st century, and the gradual restructuring of human society under the control of World Government, had gone a long way towards aping those criteria that the Anunnaki had wished to instil in their offspring.

Daniel's summation impressed Mark to such an extent that he almost forgot the most important question of all which was where the Anunnaki were likely to land upon their return to Earth, and how would such an unimaginable event be perceived by humanity as a whole.

Again, Daniel responded in his usual precise way, by quoting something that Adapa had told him a long time ago, namely that previous landings had, in the main, occurred in the Southern Hemisphere and would in all probability continue to be so again, with Ley lines with their associated electrical and magnetic forces used to guide the space ships, and with the ancient pyramids of Southern Mexico, Southern Egypt and China acting as "destination" beacons.

At this point their discussions were interrupted by the arrival of Andrew Shafter, who having received Mark's message –"Daniel is back" had journeyed to Brisbane.

CHAPTER NINTEEN

With Margaret having taken Daniel on a sightseeing tour of Brisbane, Sam, Mark Andrews and Andrew Shafter reconvened in Mark's office where Sam proceeded to up-date Andrew of his experiences over the last forty eight hours in the presence of the Anu, and the information that he had obtained, via Daniel, of the imminent return of the Anunnaki to planet Earth.

Three main issues occupied their subsequent conversation, all of which were considered as being of paramount importance to advising World Government of probable future events and the return of the Gods.

The first related to how and when the world at large should be told of the discovery in 2107 of a young man, born at the turn of the century, who through possessing an unique genome, had extraordinary psychokinetic, telekinetic, teleportation and ESP abilities, enabling him to communicate with extraterrestrials from the planet Nibiru, whose existence had been confirmed towards the end of the 21st century.

Secondly, and as a consequence of this communication, it was highly probable that Earth would be re-visited by the extraterrestrial Anunnaki from this recently discovered planet, sometime during 2112, and that the authorities, if not the population as a whole would have to be informed.

Thirdly, that all the evidence obtained so far, indicated that the Anunnaki were the creators of humankind, having first visited planet earth 450,000 years previously, and that their imminent visit was one of many that had taken place at 4,500 year intervals when the 4,500 year elliptical orbit of Nibiru around the Sun brought it to its nearest point to earth.

It was also clear that these visits had a purpose, namely the long-term commitment to monitor the development and progress of humankind whose creation had been possible by skilful genetical engineering involving the introduction of genetic material from the Anunnaki genetic pool into the genome of an existing earth-bound *primate*.

As the Minister with responsibility for World Population Trends and Development, Andrew Shafter considered his first responsibility was to inform his colleagues who collectively formed the World Parliament and whose responsibilities included not only the education, health and social welfare of society, but for those aspects of research and development, communication, transport, manufacturing, business and the protection, that impinged on individuals and societies as a whole.

In this context, he felt that further delays in making known the discoveries, first prompted by the Daniel's unique genome and extraordinary abilities, and culminating with Daniel and his foster parents being abducted by the Anunnaki, and returning to earth with the news that the return of the Gods was imminent, would not be advisable and should be made known to society in general so that a strategy could be put in place to welcome the visitors.

While Mark and Sam agreed that such information had to be made public in the longer term, the methodology of its release was in their opinion crucial.

The development of quantum computing, with speeds a hundred times faster than the Broadband of the early 21st century, the introduction of Internet terminals into every household, coupled with strict State control of all web material and information available, had resulted in an advanced society where media control was central to all developments.

Although this development had removed public exposure to undesirable websites, advertising, false information and extreme opinions, it had resulted in a society very much protected from all forms of extremes, and the danger that information relating to an alien invasion, or similar event, had to be considered carefully since it might well precipitate panic, as portrayed in many old science fiction films like H G Well's *War of the Worlds*.

On the other hand, the population as a whole had become more educated as a result of IVF and IVE provision with its associated genetic screening and remedial engineering to remove unfavourable characteristics and genetic-induced illnesses, while the follow-on programmes of education and training geared to the genetic orientation and wishes of the individual, had ensured that acceptable levels of literacy, numeracy and general education applied to all.

High profile technological developments such as the launching of satellites, the building of space laboratories and regular manned and unmanned missions to the Moon, had also made society much more aware of the possibilities of the existence of other life-forms elsewhere in the universe.

While these conditions applied to main-stream society, there was still the question of how those thousands of families in Type 2 Reservations who, through choice, had opted out of main-stream choosing to follow a more traditional way of life more in keeping with the latter part of the 20th century, should be told.

Although regulated in terms of being housed in State accommodation, with imposed travel restrictions, and only being allowed one child per couple, the traditional parenting of that child often included a religious input, with many families still practising the basics of one of the once dominant religions of the world, all of which were based on the teachings of a

"God" and the promise that such gods would one day return.

Consideration as to how these social groups would receive the news was also imperative, if social unrest was to be avoided.

There was then the question as to what form this visitation would take since although Daniel had told Sam that this would occur, he had given no details as to what form this would take. Would it take the form of a fleet of space craft entering the Earth's atmosphere, selecting a landing site and then establishing a base-camp? Would it take the form of one or two space vehicles landing in remote regions where their presence would be hard to detect and monitor? Would they take the form of the unidentified flying objects or flying saucers which had been seen by many during times of Global conflict? Would the visitors, as Daniel predicted and from the evidence provided by both Margaret and Sam during their meeting with Anu, be friendly, with their main wish being to help human beings create a better world?

These were questions that all three men recognised would be asked of them, once this amazing news was known to the world.

CHAPTER TWENTY

It was late evening before Sam was able to join Daniel and Margaret, and since it had been agreed that his discussions with Mark and Andrew would continue the following day, an over-night stay at the World Genetics Centre had been arranged.

Once settled in the two bedroom apartment provided, and having had a meal in the Centre's restaurant, the following few hours were the first in days that they had a chance to relax and contemplate the details of what had been an adventure beyond their wildest dreams, and to ascertain whether Daniel had any further relevant information that he might have omitted when recalling his telepathic conversation with Anu.

As a consequence of the discussions with Mark and Andrew, Sam had mentally organised the events of the last few days, and as a result was aware that although fairly comprehensive, gaps still existed in his knowledge - gaps which he now hoped Daniel could fill.

Whether the Anunnaki would land their space ships in the conventional way or use their teleportation powers to land on earth?, whether they would use these powers to abduct humans for interrogation and screening, as they had done with him and Margaret, thus removing the need to physically land, or would their visit include a walk among their creation were all questions, that in Sam's opinion, were crucial to how the visit should be portrayed to the population as a whole.

Who might be their targets for abduction? How would they communicate with those abducted should telepathy prove to be non-viable? Once having the information that they required, what did they hope to achieve? Would they help mankind towards a better life? Would there be anger with the failings of their creation, or pleasure with its progress since their last visit?

Daniel in his usual calm and considered way, attempted to deal with all Sam's questions, admitting that in most instances that he could only assume the possibilities and that right now no definitive answers could be given. He was however sure that from Anu's reaction to the information that he, Sam and Margaret had given in relation to the changes that had taken place in human society over the last hundred years, that it had been well received, and that the developments in genetic engineering and social engineering had been looked on favourably, and as contributing towards removing some of the imperfections of humankind.

At this point Sam had to be satisfied, and they all retired for what they hoped would be a good night's sleep.

The following morning an excited Daniel woke up Sam and Margaret with the news that Adapa had visited him during the night, and had told him that the Anunnaki would be re-visiting Earth on the 12th day of the 12th month of the 12th year of the 22nd century of the Linnaeus Calendar. Although he was unsure of the exact location of their landing, he was fairly certain that the old "markers", and Ley-lines used in previous visits would still be the guidelines to establish a correct orbit of the earth, even if not for an actual landing.

Adapa had also informed Daniel that the *Gods* wished him to be involved in their visit as a means of providing a communication-link that his unique ESP and multi-lingual abilities made possible. Anu had also indicated that his presence would also facilitate explanations for those aspects of human behaviour and developments which in many instances were not observable features.

This information was beyond Sam's wildest dreams, and following a hurried breakfast of fruit juice and cereals he hurried off to Mark Andrews' office to break the news.

In the presence of Mark and Andrew, Sam announced that on the 12/12/2112 the *Creators* would return and the promise made to humankind some 4,500 years previously, and which was recorded in practically all the old religious teachings, would be kept.

The imminent nature of this event resulted in further discussions being curtailed, with Andrew Shafter making hurried plans to return to his headquarters and to report to his World Government colleagues, Mark Andrews to preparing a written report on the events to date, while Sam having decided that there was no further reason to remain in Brisbane, contacting his X33 pilot James, for an immediate return flight to Valencia.

Once settled on the plane Sam and Margaret settled down to discuss the amazing events of the last few days since they left Valencia, while Daniel as per usual was on the flight deck discussing with James and Antonio the rout of their return flight and their estimated time of arrival.

Margaret's main concerns, which Sam realised were of long standing, centered on the enormous power that the Anunnaki obviously had at their disposal, and its possible use should there be conflict between the visitors and those experienced, highly intelligent individuals, who through a genetically engineered extended life-span, now formed the World Government.

These individuals who over the last twenty five years had given enormous service to humanity as a whole, had essentially rescued the world from the ongoing pattern of conflicts, destruction and miseries as depicted by two World Wars, numerous other military conflicts, hunger and starvation, world-wide terrorism, and in the early and middle part of the 21st century, economic greed and the eventual meltdown of financial structures, mass economic migration, racial tensions, and the eventual collapse of sovereign states and democratic institutions.

In Margaret's opinion these humans would not take kindly to being told what to do, or forced to take action against their will, although she felt that within all mankind there still lingered the belief of a good and kind *God* who fathered mankind.

Another unknown factor was in relation to the number of Anunnaki who would visit Earth, since during their meetings with Anu there had been no other presence, and with the exception of Adapa, no other mention had been made by Daniel. Would the visitors be of mixed gender or were the Anunnaki a race that had evolved through a process of cloning? Would they therefore all resemble Anu? Would their powers of telepathy enable them to read human thoughts as was the case with Daniel? These were all questions that Margaret felt should be addressed at the earliest opportunity.

CHAPTER TWENTY ONE

Once back in Valencia, Daniel announced that he would like to see Professor Poveda and would Sam make arrangements for him to continue with his painting tutorials to her home at an early date. Mindful of the roll Regina had played in informing Mark of their whereabouts following their abduction by the Anunnaki, Sam had no hesitation in complying with his wishes, and within minutes he was speaking to Regina, before handing over his qPhone to Daniel who excitedly told her he was back in Valencia, would like to continue with his tutorials, and was very sorry if his note had given her cause for concern, but that she was the only one that he could trust with such information. Having fixed a date for his visit, Daniel handed back Sam's qPhone saying "You know Uncle Sam I like Professor Poveda very much."

Sam then settled down to prepare the written report of the events leading up to, during, and following their abduction by the Anunnaki. This had been requested by both Mark Andrews and Andrew Shafter and would form the basis of Andrew's formal report to the World Parliament which would bring to its attention the fact that through a young boy with an unique genome resulting in unique psychokinetic and extra sensory abilities, communication had been established with extra terrestrials, who 450,000 years previously had been responsible for the creation of humankind on earth, and who would shortly be re-visiting earth.

Margaret busied herself in catching up with her domestic duties before visiting the local super market for some essential commodities. Although the majority of families used their Web connection to order and get their shopping delivered, Margaret in the main still adopted the old fashion method of visiting the local shop in person since, as she explained, she preferred speaking to an assistant face to face rather than through a web monitor. She also liked to see and handle what she was buying, rather than view a picture on a screen.

In keeping with normal practice she was accompanied by Daniel who appeared to gain much pleasure in such visits, taking every opportunity to chat with the locals who Margaret was acquainted with. Many such locals had noted his absence over the past eighteen months and enquired as to the welfare of his family in South America. Although Daniel was well aware that this was a cover-story he responded in his usual courteous manner thanking them for their enquiry and indicating that all was well with his family and that he was very pleased to be back in Valencia.

Hearing these conversations Margaret was struck by the maturity that Daniel had acquired during the last eighteen months with the Anunnaki, and although since their very first meeting in New Mexico, she had been aware of a maturity far beyond his years, he had now made further exceptional progress and was showing characteristics of a mature, highly intelligent and understanding adult who had a natural instinct for the feelings of his fellow human beings.

Did he have other as yet undiscovered talents; was a question that Margaret kept asking herself, since in her opinion human beings had a long way to go if they were to eventually attain parity with their creators.

Two days later saw Sam, with an excited Daniel in the passenger seat, driving out of Valencia and heading for the orange groves of Monte Picio and the villa of Professor Regina Poveda.

Their reunion was an emotional one with a smiling Regina meeting them outside the villa and throwing her arms around Daniel and hugging him with tears of joy glinting in her dark eyes. Then turning to Sam she whispered in her soft unmistakable Spanish accent, "I am so happy to see you again and to know that you are all safe".

The next few hours were spent with Daniel recalling his experiences of their abduction, time in the presence of Anu on board the space ship, and concluding with the news of the impending visitation to earth. Regina sat enthralled listening to this amazing account, her eyes never leaving his face, while her thoughts raced forward to the possible implications of what she was being told on human society in general.

Although in her opinion, similar visits had undoubtedly occurred in the distant past, increased understanding of the world, knowledge relating to the number of planets in the universe, and the probability of there being intelligent life on at least some of these planets, made possible through higher levels of intellect among the population of the 22nd century, would enable humankind to understand, portray, and respond to such an event, in a way very different from the recordings by primitive man in ancient cuneiform writings, drawings and other art forms, which scholars throughout the centuries had translated as the *Gods* visiting human kind.

When Daniel had finished his account, Regina turned to Sam and asked "What happens now?"

Sam's considered response was "We sit a wait and hope that the news, as and when it is released through the World Government's web site, and enters every household, will not generate panic, and will be seen by palaeontologists, anthropologists, scientists and the public in general, as the final chapter of evidence in determining the origin and subsequent evolution of modern humans."

Regina's next question took Sam completely by surprise. "What proof have we got that makes us believe that the Anunnaki are not already with us?"

This was a scenario that until that moment had not crossed Sam's mind, and the very possibility as posed by the question, sent his thoughts racing, as he recalled the initial *link* between Daniel and Adapa who, as far as he could ascertain, was a *messenger* of the Anunnaki, and during his numerous conversations with Daniel had prepared him for his meeting with Anu, and their eventual meeting with Anu.

Observing Sam's reaction, Regina continued "You know that over the last century there have been many theories that propound the existence of extraterrestrials living with us on earth, but that we were unaware of their existence since externally they resemble humans."

"Others propound that they exist as *spirits* only detected by those human beings with some ESP abilities."

Although Sam recalled numerous conversations with Margaret relating to such possibilities, he had been taken by surprise by Regina's questions and responded by saying "I think that you and Margaret should get together on this, since she would love to share and talk-through her thoughts on ESP with a kindred spirit."

Hearing this conversation, Daniel butted in by saying "Please Professor Regina do come and visit us in Valencia we would love to see you."

CHAPTER TWENTY TWO

The establishment of a World Government consisting of individuals with specialist knowledge in the various sectors of government, and an understanding of the cultural needs of the various geographical regions, coupled with the experience gained by the suppression of the ageing gene, and a long life expectancy, had been a long and difficult process.

The concept of national co-operation had been established during the second decade of the 21st century, and as a consequence of a world financial crisis in 2008/2009 brought about by reckless lending by poorly regulated banks and inherent human greed. The resulting restrictions on all forms of credit, plunged world commerce into a deep depression, which in turn brought about, social unrest due to the lack of employment, made worse by previously uncontrolled economic migration with migrants perceived to being treated better than the ethnic population. This in turn led to the break up of so-called multi-ethnic societies with ghettos emerging as the alternative. The gradual break up of the traditional family unit and lack of parental guidance, had in many instances given rise to anti-social behaviour in the young, which when fuelled by religious fanatics had resulted in religion-based local and global terrorism.

Although initially, the resolution of these problems were tackled by National governments and by trading and economic partners, little success was achieved, mainly due to failure of the political systems of the time, with politicians making promises that they were unable to keep and their credibility among the population reaching an all time low. Calls for a common approach to dealing with such problems across national boundaries were hampered by national and territorial interest, which were essentially a throw-back to the tribal and social instincts of early man, and to politicians always being mindful of the consequences should they alienate their electorate.

The first stage in the de-politicising of the existing systems of government in the majority of countries was through the recruitment of highly qualified, intelligent and internationally successful men and women into government positions. The second and equally important stage was in the governments gaining of control of the media and banning all forms of advertising, removing false and misleading information from the Web, coupled with its introduction into all majority of homes world wide, and the uniformity of the international education and training provision for all young people up to the age of 18.

This latter programme, coupled with the development of genetic screening of all embryos that many national governments had already introduced, had the gradual effect of enhancing human health and intelligence, and eliminating many undesirable antisocial characteristics.

The initial format of World Government was based on the United Nations concept established during the mid twentieth century following the Second World War, with the UN Security Council forming the Executive with the position of President, elected by members of that Executive. It was this basic concept of international co-operation taken to its logical conclusion that had resulted in a World Governing Body being established in 2085, with the initial task of making the world a safer and more secure place, and ensuring that there were the same levels of individual opportunity across all the geographical regions.

The initial objective was achieved by strict arms control, the apprehension of those individuals with proven terrorist and criminal tendencies, and their incarceration in high security Reservations spread around the globe. These reservations also catered for those already in prisons and remand centres which were eventually closed. A second type of Reservations with a low security presence was also established to cater for those who, by choice, had opt-out of main stream society and wished to pursue a more traditional existence although under strict controls including travel restrictions.

The equalisation of social opportunity had been a more difficult target, which had only been possible by the gradual improvement in the levels of education and training of the population in general, strict control of the birth rate with a restriction of one child per partnership, the control and eventual disbanding of international companies in favour of regional enterprises catering for the needs of a specified geographical area, and hence removing the need for trans-global transportation of commodities, with a resulting saving of energy and the stabilisation of global warming. This latter development involved a massive injection of government funding for the under developed geographical regions to bring about global parity and to make them attractive to the indigenous population who had previously been forced to seek a better life in the more prosperous regions, to return to their homeland.

This massive exercise in social engineering had not been achieved without cost, with countless dissidents being killed or confined indefinitely to reservations, and with very many freedoms that had been enjoyed by the majority of world population in the early part of the 21st century being lost as a consequence of the need to curtail the greed, religious fanaticism, and power seeking actions, of a minority.

In terms of functioning, world government operated within five geographical regions – North and South America, European, Chinese, Indian /African, and Australasia. Each region had an appointed Vice-President who was a member of the Executive, while within each region there were Area Chairpersons with responsibility for the governance of that particular geographical area.

While this geographical division ensured domestic governance, a matrix provision consisting of seven Executive members (Ministers) with Global responsibilities, ensured that all regions and areas conformed to the approved policy relating to - Population Security, Population Trends and Development, Global Aviation and Transport, Global Finance and Financial Control, Global Industry and Commerce, Global Environmental and Global Media and News Networking.

It was to this highest tier of government, meeting at its Beijing head quarters and involving the Vice Presidents and Ministers under the chairmanship of the President that the Minister for Population Trends and Development Andrew Shafter, reported.

CHAPTER TWENTY THREE

As the discussions relating to what was now known as the *Daniel Project* commenced in Beijing, so an excited Daniel was greeting Professor Poveda as she paid her first visit to the apartment in Valencia.

As the years had rolled by, Regina Poveda had, in the eyes of many, become somewhat of a recluse, spending much of her time at her villa, surrounded by her paintings, books and artefacts of the past. Although she still made the occasional visit to her beloved museum and Art gallery, a social visit such as the one she was now undertaking was a rare event.

After exchanging pleasantries with Margaret, and commenting as to how nice the apartment was, Daniel insisted that she should view his drawings and art work that he had in his bedroom, and taking her by the hand he proudly led the way, to where on his bedside desk was an array of pencil sketches and half finished paintings. Studying the numerous sketches reminded Regina of the work of Leonardo Da Vince with sketches of helicopters, planes, and other forms of flying vehicles drawn hundreds of years before their existence. Indeed there were numerous similarities, but what struck her most forcibly was the skill exhibited in the drawings, skills that she had already detected in the oil painting of Anu that Daniel had made following his first visit to the Anunnaki space ship.

After Daniel had explained the origin of his ideas for the sketches and Regina had complimented him on his skills as an artist, she made her escape to join Margaret and to discuss the issues that Sam had considered was worthy of their joint input when considering the implications of the impending visit by the Anunnaki.

Both women acknowledged that throughout thousands of years of history, biblical and historical references had been made to "flaming chariots", huge flying "birds" and the existence of odd looking beings. In more recent times some authorities believed that alien space craft had been recovered and that human-looking aliens had made contact with Governments warning humanity that it should destroy its nuclear weapons, stop wars and the killing of each other, stop polluting the earth, stop raping the earth's natural resources and learn to live in harmony with one another.

All such references had not however been confirmed by any government, and if genuine, had not been made known to the population at large, although speculation from time to time had been rife, with permanent committees such as "Majority Twelve" (MJ12) supposedly overseeing covert activities between the USA and aliens.

The idea that aliens had manipulated and/or ruled the human race since its creation, through various secret societies, religions and the occult, had over the centuries been regarded as a distinct possibility, with the information in the possession of such organisations, a carefully guarded secret. These forces had undoubtedly contributed to, and influenced the development of technology during the latter part of the 20th century and throughout the 21st century, and to a lesser extent had in all probability contributed to shaping human society in general over the millennia.

What had not been considered seriously, in Margaret's opinion, was the genetic-link between such forces and the initial donation of genetic material by the creators of the human race, a link that would eventually give humans these superhuman qualities that they had always craved for.

Although not a geneticist, Regina had always taken a keen interest in   world affairs, and the changes that had occurred over the last century, in terms of art, literature and basic human values. These changes, on a wider front, had culminated in the establishment of World Government, a world money system, universal currency, and a uniformity, that had in many ways had enslaved the world's population, and in other ways curtailed individual ambition. Although she could fully understand the reasons why such development had occurred, and welcomed it's success in removing ethnic and religious terrorism, stabilising the world's population, conserving the earth's energy resources, reducing global warming, and equalling the quality of life for millions of people, she had always pondered as to whether this responding to need was the ultimate goal for humanity, or was it part of a great plan.

Were all these developments influenced by those genes introduced by the Anunnaki onto chromosome 4 and 17 and, as in the case of Daniel, had given selected humans the ability to communicate with the extraterrestrial Anunnaki and learn more of their technology and their ambitions for the human race?

There was also the question as to whether throughout history, certain humans as a consequence of their genetic makeup had the ability to communicate with extraterrestrials like Adapa, or had in some way experienced abduction of one kind or another.

The fact that throughout the last two centuries, millions of individuals had disappeared without trace was in Regina's opinion, worthy of further consideration.

Were these individuals abducted, but unlike Daniel, never returned? Where there other aliens visiting and monitoring the development of humanity on earth, in addition to the Anunnaki? With the current estimate of around 361 of the 37,900 planets in the galaxy deemed capable of supporting some life forms, this assumption was reasonably realistic, with the existence of both good and evil life forms a possibility.

These exchanges and the questions posed, was as Sam had predicted, extremely stimulating to both Margaret and Regina, and their conversation would have continued for hours but for Regina declaring that she must return home before dark, and Daniel making an appearance stating that he was hungry, and bringing a touch of reality to the proceedings.

After Regina had taken her leave, inviting both Margaret and Daniel to visit her soon, and promising that she would keep in touch regarding the issues they had discussed, Margaret set about preparing the evening meal for her and Daniel. Following the meal during which time Daniel expressed his fondness for Regina, a sentiment endorsed by Margaret, the evening was soon over, with Daniel retiring for the night, while Margaret sat out on the balcony overlooking Valencia, slowly sipping what was left of the wine she had opened for the meal.

As she sat gazing out over the lights of the city, her thoughts returned to that afternoon's conversation with Regina and the question, - Had an alien presence always existed on earth?

CHAPTER TWENTY FOUR

The establishment of a World Governing Body had been a long and torturous process and its formal establishment in 2085 had been the most important human achievement of the 21st century.

It's existence was due mainly to the need to combat forces which collectively had made some form of global control essential and inevitable, while its functioning had only been possible as a consequence of the strides made in human genetics by the suppression of the ageing gene that had resulted in individuals with a greatly extended life-span, creating a pool of knowledge and experience appropriate to dealing with recurring global problems.

One of the many problems initially encountered by both National governments and International organisations during the early part of the 21st century was in relation to the need of supporting professional politicians with men and women deemed experts in their particular field. Such recruitment of experts with sufficient knowledge but with no subsequent conflict of interests had proven very difficult.

It was only the recruitment of individuals with the experience and expertise, who had relinquished involvement with current developments in their field, yet through experience and hindsight, resulting from genetically engineered long levity, could advise dispassionately on current difficulties and initiate action, that this problem was overcome.

The gradual demise of political parties, professional politicians, and National governments brought about by a combination of greed, corruption and loss of public trust, completed the transition from democratically elected representation to governance by *elders* chosen by their peers, who collectively were responsible for all the various facets of global governance.

It was to his fellow *elders* that Andrew Shafter as Minister with responsibility for Population Trends and Development presented his report outlining the facts and implications of the *Daniel Project*.

As anticipated, the report that had been jointly prepared by Sam, Mark Andrews and Andrew Shafter, and which identified the existence of a genome which gave the individual superhuman abilities including the ability to communicate and converse with the extraterrestrial Anunnaki, coupled with the news that Sam's X33 had been abducted by the Anunnaki during its flight to Brisbane, and that upon their return they were able to report that the Anunnaki intended to return to earth after a period of 4,500 years, on the 12/12/2112, caused unprecedented concerns and discussion among the *elders*, and the debate that followed contained several facets for consideration.

It had become obvious to the Ministry for Population Security, which was responsible for both military and civil policing, that over the years the possibility of an alien presence on earth did exist. Many theories had been advanced ranging from the suggestion that alien bases had been constructed underground in some of the American States during the latter end of the 20th century, on the pretext that they were for the President of the United States and his staff should a nuclear conflict ever occur, to the theory that alien beings were already among the population influencing society as and when possible. Although the Department of Population Security had been in existence for twenty five years, there were many facets of previous national administrations that were still unclear due to destroyed records and secrecy among staff that had left those administrations, but were still complying with the official secrets Act.

Against this background and its logistical difficulties, a full investigation had moved down the priority list of the department with other more pressing issues such as the eradication of global terrorism, the repatriation of ethnic minorities and the control of racial conflict, and the establishment of Type 1 Reservations as an alternative to prisons and remand centres, had been given top priority.

Another major debating issue was the image of the Anunnaki, as interpreted and created by various authors and historians throughout the ages. Although the name was believed to have originated from the word Anunnaka which related to group of Sumerian and Akkadian deities who were apparently related to the Annuna (the Great Gods), up until the present time, and the events surrounding Daniel, there had been no proof of their extraterrestrial origins, the existence of the planet Nibiru, or that they were the genetic manipulators who created human kind.

Zecharia Sitchin's book *The Twelfth Planet*, fathered subsequent writings relating to the Anunnaki and their role in the development of human kind, while the subsequent discovery of the planet Nibiru towards the end of the 21st century, and the mapping of its orbit within the solar system suggesting an elliptical orbit with a trajectory resulting in its being at the closest point to earth occurring once every 4,500 years, gave such speculative writings greater credence in relation to periodic visits to earth by the Anunnaki and to the concept that they were the creators of humankind. The fact that there was now confirmed evidence that this was indeed concept was correct and that the Anunnaki would be returning to earth on the 12/12/2112 was, even to the elders a situation with no precedent and one that they recognised would require all their skill and knowledge when releasing such information the population at large.

Researching all that had been written about the Anunnaki, there was little doubt in the minds of the *elders* that they were a technologically advanced alien race, with a civilisation that identified them as elite. Their existence had been recorded in Babylonian mythology with Anu and Ki, brother and sister gods being responsible for the creation of humankind. This mythology also referred to the head of the Anunnaki as the Great Anu rather than being just a sky god. Religious writings as in the Bible's Old Testament refer to the Anunnaki as the Anakim, "heavenly" visitors or "those who came from heaven to earth". Other writings identified them as biological beings with abounding pride, arrogance and a great appetite for conquest and control, and with an oppressive cast and gender system which could be regarded as misogynistic.

It was against this background of myths and ancient writings that the events that had been recorded and verified in the *Daniel Project* were considered by the *elders* of the World Government.

After many hours of debate it was decided that a communiqué would be issued via the Web to the population at large informing them that communication had been established with an extraterrestrial race known as the Anunnaki, and that evidence existed confirming the Anunnaki as being the genetic manipulators who around 450,000 years previously had engineered humankind.

CHAPTER TWENTY FIVE

Monday the twelfth of December 2112 dawned bright and sunny in Valencia. Sam had visited his old department at Oxford the previous week, and as always had discussed ongoing investigations involving Daniel with Julie and Paul, while ensuring that he kept well clear of the acting director Edward Chapman, who according to Paul was not very pleased at being side-lined by Mark Andrews when it came to information relating to the *Daniel Project*. He had however been informed that the project was being considered by the Council of World Ministers and that a communiqué would be issued shortly. Sam for his part had been very diplomatic in all his discussions with Julie and Paul, although since he regarded them as friends in addition to work colleagues, he had indicated that there had been a significant development in the *Daniel Project* and that they should watch out for information in the form of a Government communiqué on or around the 12th December.

As he showered and dressed that morning, Sam recalled the events of the past years – events that previously would not have been part of his wildest dreams. His very first meeting with Daniel on the reservation in New Mexico where he lived with his parents, the tragic events that resulted in the death of both his mother and father, and his subsequent adoption by Margaret and himself.

Then the discoveries relating to the boy's unique genome linked to his superhuman abilities in psychokinetic, telekinetic and teleportation skills, which had resulted in his eventual communication with the Anunnaki, and through psychoportation had firstly resulted in his disappearance into their world, and later, upon his return to earth resulted in the abduction of their flight from Valencia to Brisbane and their meeting with Anu an *elder* of the Anunnaki. Finally, their release from the space ship by Anu, and their return to earth with news that the Anunnaki intended to return to earth on the 12th December 2112 after a gap of around 4,500 earth years.

Since their return to earth and the debriefing at the meeting with Mark Andrews and Andrew Shafter, Sam had spent the major part of his time researching all the information and speculative writings available on the Anunnaki, and relating what he discovered to the meetings, and communication through Daniel, that he had with Anu during his and Margaret's abduction onto the spaceship.

This mythical alien race known to the ancient people of earth as the Anunnaki were believed to come from the planet Nibiru which originated from another solar system but with an orbit that brought it close to earth once every 3,600 to 4,500 years. It was this orbit, and the possession of an advanced technology that allowed the Anunnaki to observe and investigate planets such as earth as the planet Nibiru travelled through space like a mobile observatory.

The earliest reference to the name Anunnaki and its literal meaning of "those who came from heaven to earth" was, Sam discovered, first recorded in the Old Testament of the Bible and its reference to "heavenly" visitors called the "Anakim".

Sam also discovered that there were various views among writers as to the characteristics of the Anunnaki but that all tended to arrive at the opinion that they were biological beings with abounding pride, arrogance and with an appetite for conquest and control brought about by their specialisation in extra sensory mind control, and their intensive knowledge of genetic engineering. During their various visits to earth, - visits that were spread over 450,000 years and only occurring when Nibiru was at its nearest point to earth; the Anunnaki had gradually developed and imposed a complex, oppressive cast and gender system on their initial creation.

There was little doubt among most authors and researchers that the Anunnaki were misogynists and that through their influence they eliminated the worship of the *Devine Mother* practiced by early humans, replacing her with *"mothers"*, *"earth mother"* or *"mother nature"* through the corruption of her image and falsely attributing her with lustful, vengeful and jealous qualities. An example of such false interpretation was exemplified by the case of the Hindu goddess *Kali,* where the original belief that she was the goddess of time and change was corrupted to represent a goddess of annihilation, death and destruction.

Through genetic engineering, women were made physically inferior to men in stature, strength and speed of movement and even in activities where such characteristics were irrelevant were greatly disadvantaged.

There was also significant evidence that the Anunnaki during their latter visits to earth created many religions which was used as a powerful means of controlling humanity.

The initial geographical separation of warring fractions or races of humanity by the Anunnaki, coupled with genetic labelling introduced to distinguish the various groups, was further targeted by the setting up of different religions with doctrines in direct opposition to one another in order to breed disharmony, distrust, confusion and war and through such agencies keep the various fractions apart.

In all such religions the misogynistic influence of the Anunnaki could be identified, with any attempt to attribute good in women played down. This chauvinism resulted in the subjugation of women to men in numerous regions of the world, with many cultures including the Arab, Asian, Jewish treating women as inferior beings.

As Sam recalled from his days as a youth growing up in the UK society of the early part of the 21st century, Christian teachings including the teachings of the Old Testament and the teachings of Paul, subordinated all Christian women to an inferior status, and while their gradual emergence as equals to men in the Protestant church had taken place during the latter end of the 20th century and early 21st century, the Roman Catholic church with Paul being its first Pope, was far more reluctant to accede to such development with there being no women priests until the latter end of the 21st century, when all religions were loosing their influence.

The Anunnaki were also accredited with creating and promoting myths throughout the various geographical/ethnic groups of humans, with the various religions, and accompanying myths, aimed at controlling and manipulating the populations.

These religions were not based upon love, but upon fear. The gradual organisation of humans into communities where control in terms of physical, emotional, mental, spiritual, and economical needs was easier to ensure, was also a tool encouraged by the Anunnaki, as was the need to keep the majority of humans ignorant of their environment, potential power and latent abilities.

There were many other aspects of Anunnaki influence which humans had either copied or inherited, including the adornment of the body with jewellery and

117

precious gems, polygamy, incest and paedophilia which were traits in various cultures, including the Sumerians and ancient Egyptian cultures. The Sumerian culture, according to many authors, did not evolve over many thousand of years, but was introduced by the Anunnaki to include a legal system, social order, economic models, religion, science, mathematics, weights and measures, writing, literature, music, the performing arts, cosmology, painting, sculpture, astronomy, astrology, medicine, animal husbandry, domestication of plants, homeopathy, culinary skills, art, and entertainment. With this background, much of which had been confirmed by Daniel during his ESP sessions with Adapa and Anu, Sam could but wonder what the Anunnaki would make of the world and its inhabitants in 2112.

CHAPTER TWENTY SIX

As Sam entered the lounge having showered and dressed, and having collected his morning glass of freshly squeezed orange juice from the kitchen, he was greeted by Margaret who, still in her night attire, was seated in front of the quantum computer screen that occupied a prominent position in their living accommodation.

"The communiqué by the government has just been put up on the web" she announced. "Come and have a look and see what you make of it".

In keeping with all public information communiqués issued by the World Government, it was short and succinct, reading as follows:-

"The Council wishes to announce that a communications link has been established with extraterrestrials. An alien group, known as the Anunnaki, and believed to come from the planet Nibiru, which was discovered by space telescope technology during the latter part of the 21st century, have made contact through a human being and indicated their intention to visit Earth in the near future.

All the indications are that the Anunnaki are an advanced humanoid race possessing an advanced form of technology, and their visit, which is believed to be one of many that have occurred in the distant past, may well benefit humanity. People of Earth should not feel threatened."

As Sam read the missive he could but wonder at what the general public's response would be, since although a great deal had been written and filmed about alien visitors from space, space travel and the discovery of alien cultures on other planets, these had all been science fiction written by authors with vivid imaginations, and in many instances their conversion into images by cinematic technology had been designed to frighten and create a memorable spectacle. Would this news of impending alien visitors be categorised in the minds of the public in the same way?

At this point his thoughts were interrupted by Daniel entering the lounge. Already showered and dressed with his hair carefully combed and his olive skin glistening in the morning sunlight, he looked a picture of health and vitality, while his grown-up appearance and dark smiling eyes were always a source of pleasure to both Sam and Margaret. "Good morning aunty Margaret and uncle Sam what's new?" Pointing to the screen, Sam commented "The news that your friends the Anunnaki are coming, has just been announced." "I already knew that" said Daniel, "Adapa told me when he visited me last night to let me know that Anu wants me to join him as soon as possible."

Sam and Margaret exchanging glances, responded in unison, "Where have they landed?"

"According to Adapa, the actual landing site is about a hundred miles from the population centre of Nazca in South America, and close to the Peruvian coast line."

"From his description it must be near that region that we flew over when we visited those ancient civilization sites in South America and close to where James our pilot, pointed out the 595 foot high "Candelabra of the Andes" which he reckoned was some form of flight path if you were trying to land from the air. You remember Uncle Sam!"

Recalling what he had read of Geoglyphs World wide Sam immediately knew the location Daniel was referring to, since that particular region was scattered with drawings of llamas, birds, fish, and in the Solitary region the world's largest human figure known as the "Giant of Atacama" standing some 393 feet high at Cerro Unitas. If what Daniel had just said was correct, then in Sam's view the prediction by Erich von Daniken's back in the 20th century, in his book "Arrival of the Gods", was turning out to be correct.

Following breakfast, Margaret busied herself with the washing up and the usual tidying of the apartment, while Sam with one eye on the Web Access screen, read over some of the notes that he had brought back from Oxford following his last visit there. Daniel meanwhile returned to his room mentioning that there was something he needed to do.

As mid-day approached, the Web screen suddenly went dead, and Sam's qphone ceased to function as he discovered when he attempted to contact his neighbour to find out whether his Web was working, and that it was a local fault. Since such a communications blackout was very rare and practically unheard of in recent times, Sam went out onto the balcony to check whether there were any other signs that this blackout was being experienced by the city as a whole. All appeared normal, although the few pedestrians that he could see from his lofty perch above the street
appeared to be having problems with their qPhones, which, like his own, were displaying blank screens.

At this point Margaret joined him on the balcony, and when he told her of the non-functioning of the Web and qPhone, her response was immediate, "Does this not remind you of when we were abducted by the Anunnaki on our flight to Brisbane when all the communication systems on the plane failed?"

Sam seeing the obvious link responded, "Are you suggesting that the World's communication systems have been decommissioned in a similar fashion by the Anunnaki?"

"I guess I am", was Margaret's response, lets see what Daniel thinks.

Leaving the balcony she tapped on Daniel's bedroom door and entered. The room was empty.

CHAPTER TWENTY SEVEN

President Dong Kurn Lee and the seven Executive members of the World Government Council representing the Ministries for Global Population and Security; Global Population Trends and Development; Global Aviation and Transport; Global Finance and Financial Control; Global Industry and Commerce; Global Environmental Control; and Global Media and News Networking who, a few hours earlier, and after hours of debate, had approved and issued the communiqué relating to the impending visit by the Anunnaki, gazed in disbelief at the blank screens that faced them as they sat round the table at their headquarters in Beijing.

At no time since its initial establishment in 2085, had the administrative centre experienced this complete failure of the quantum communications system, and the realisation that they were completely isolated in terms of normal day-to-day communication links with the five Vice-Presidents responsible for the various geographical regions, and had no means of obtaining or giving information to those regions. This communication blackout brought home to all concerned the vulnerability of their situation and how dependant they had become on this single form of communication.

The foremost question in all their minds was, whether the timing of this failure was a pure coincidence, or was it related to the impending visit by the Anunnaki. As Andrew Shafter had pointed out, the information that Sam had given him in relation to the abduction of the X33 during its flight to Brisbane, when the power supply and communication systems of the plane ceased to function, would suggest that the Anunnaki did indeed possess an advanced form of technology capable of blocking or decommissioning the quantum computing system, and/or its power supply.

The second, and even more pressing question, was what should or could they do to re-establish those communication links that they, and the World's population had come to rely on in their everyday activities? The realisation that they could not even contact the technicians who maintained the communications system in the usual manner, which was by qPhone or qMail, made the problem appear even more daunting, since no one knew exactly where, geographically, the technical personnel were based.

In addition to these obvious questions, the various members of Council had their own longer term worries and concerns.

Monty Audenart, whose responsibilities for Population Security included anti-terrorism, public security and the control of 300 Reservations world wide, could envisage major problems in relation to public order. Ed Futa, with responsibility for World Financial Control, realised that if the crashing of the quantum computing system was indeed world wide, the effect would be catastrophic.

Jonathan Majiyagbe, with responsibility for Aviation and Transport, and John Kenny, with responsibility for Industry and Commerce, also viewed the situation as having enormous destructive consequences, were it to continue for any length of time.

Most affected of all was Justina Ogunseitian who, as the member of Council with responsibility for Media and News, felt personally responsible for the highly sophisticated system of communication that she and her team had developed and established over the decades.

This system had in effect replaced the numerous other media systems that had evolved since the establishment of the Web in the 20th century, and which eventually had created a system that had brought about information anarchy, and substantiated the claims of many that the *Media were the right arm of Anarchy.*

Although the current Government-controlled information system had removed conflicting information, pornographic material, advertising, pressure selling, and financial corruption, and had greatly aided access to information to main-line society as a whole, it had resulted in a significant decline in the need for memory retention of facts and figures, since by a press of a button the required information was available with little or no need to memorise.

This decline in this human ability had not appeared to present any initial problems, but had been noted and debated by Council Members and others who had undergone suppression of the aging gene, and whose life-span was such that recall of past events, facts, figures, and experiences, was a natural part of their existence, and which allowed decisions to be taken in the context of past history and recalled experiences.

Whether this observable short-fall in recent generations, brought about by the technology replacing to a point, the need for the human brain to store vast amounts of data, coupled with the dumbing down of information giving in the education and training programmes of the young, would have a longer term adverse effect, was deemed as dependant on the supporting quantum technology.

The current failure of the system had exposed a serious vulnerability directly related to over dependence on technology.

It was at this point in their discussions that the door to the Council chamber opened and a very flustered personal assistant to the President Dong Kurn Lee entered, to announce that there were two visitors who wished to meet the Council.

Before anyone could take in the request, or respond to this unheard of situation, the tall gaunt, white haired, white-robed figure of Anu appeared in the doorway accompanied by a dark haired, brown-eyed young man, who those present instantly recognised from the various files and images that they had viewed as being Daniel, while his companion who had been depicted by Daniel in his art work, and through the brain-activity recordings taken during one of his teleportation visits and meetings with the Anunnaki, was instantly recognisable as Anu.

Daniel spoke - "Although it is not possible for Anu to communicate with you all directly due to the fact that your brains are not capable of receiving telepathic thoughts, Anu wishes me to inform you that the Anunnaki have returned to Earth and that, while he apologises for the disruption in communication, he wishes you and the people of Earth no harm, only wishing to safeguard the future of the human race that was genetically engineered by his forefathers 450,000 earth years ago, and last visited 4,500 earth years ago."

"He had hoped that during the intervening years your techno-enabled telepathy, and its links with the human brain, would have developed to an extent that through *techlepathy*, *synthetic telepathy*, or *psychotronics,* the distractions of language would have been by-passed, and that he would have been able to communicate directly with you, and indeed all humans.

This development however does not appear to have taken place, and consequently he will be using the telepathic link that he has with me, to communicate with you in the universal language now used by the people of Earth."

CHAPTER TWENTY EIGHT

The complete silence that had followed Daniel's statement was broken by Dong Kurn Lee raising to his feet and with hands outstretched moving forward to greet the two visitors. Anu and Daniel responded with the old, yet now long forgotten, traditional greeting with the hands with palms facing, held before the face and a slight bow of the head. Dong Kurn Lee then gestured Anu and Daniel towards the two chairs that President Lee's personal assistant had hurriedly brought into the Council chamber and arranged facing the Council table.

Once seated, Daniel proceeded to explain that Anu communicated with his own kind, by a process of thought transference with no specific language involved.

Languages, as Anu had explained to Daniel, were the inventions of the human species, and although in the written / symbolic form had merit in recording past historical events, as a means of communication, were clumsy, easily misunderstood, and constantly changing over the millennia, with different languages evolving in different social groups throughout the world. Although initially implanted in the human genome, the emergence of telekinetic, telepathic and abilities of thought- transference had been infrequent in the species as a whole, with Daniel being the most recent example.

Human history was however littered with examples of similar individuals, with so called *prophets* of their time, conveying their thoughts, dreams and, in some instances, instructions and guidance to their fellow humans.

Following this brief introduction, Daniel proceeded to explain that this was the eleventh visit to earth by the Anunnaki. The first visitation had taken place roughly 450,000 earth years previously, at which time the first genetical engineering work was carried out on a species of the Earth's primates, which themselves had evolved through natural selection, over thousands of millennia.

The basis of this engineering technique involved the initial removal or suppression of around twenty percent of primate DNA, identified as being inappropriate in terms of the characteristics produced, and the introduction of an equivalent amount of DNA from the Anunnaki genetic bank.   The aim being to create a species with the necessary physical attributes to exist within the gravitational conditions on earth and being able to compete with the other earth species, yet possessing a genetical capability of developing mental faculties commensurate with that of their creators.

In genetical terms, the 24 pairs of chromosomes present in the primate host were reduced to 23, with much of the Anunnaki DNA introduced on chromosomes 4 and 17.

Since this donor DNA, if not suppressed, would give the recipient powers beyond that which was deemed appropriate at that stage in its development, the genes were rendered inactive through their position or loci on the various chromosomes.

Characteristics resulting from the donor DNA would only appear in   individuals following a long period of breeding within the species, with the inevitably random combinations of DNA within the genome, eventually resulting in the genes assuming the correct loci, and resulting in a random number of individuals, exhibiting mental powers, specific skills and knowledge, commensurate with the DNA implanted by the Anunnaki 450,000 years earlier.

The appearance of such individuals over the millennia was testament to the skill of the initial genetic engineering process carried out by the Anunnaki, with the most recent example being Daniel, who now acting as the voice-piece of Anu.

The first part of Anu's address to the World Council was in the form of an explanation as to why a block had been imposed on the World's communication system. The removal of this computer-generated system, used throughout the World, would not only bring home to the Council and humanity in general, the vulnerability of this form of communication, which the species had come to rely on, and took for granted, but would also show how important it was that an alternative system of communication be developed, using the inbuilt potential that existed in all human beings.

Mindful of the developments that had already been achieved in the field of human genetics, and as illustrated by the suppression of the ageing process and the elimination of numerous genetically related diseases, Anu voiced the opinion that as a consequence of the established genetic screening of embryos both in main-stream society and on reservations, coupled with the on-going study of Daniel's genome, and related brain activity, further genetic engineering by leading geneticists, could replicate genomes that would eventually produce the next stage in the evolution of human kind.

Anu then went on to express his concerns at the changes that had taken place in human society since his last visit approximately 4,500 earth years ago. The primate species initially engineered by the Anunnaki was a social animal living in a community, with a well defined social order observed by the community as a whole. This genetical trait that had been retained, and to some degree enhanced in the human genome, was considered crucial in the upbringing of the young of the species, where, due to numerous other factors the length of time between birth and independence from the parent was considerable. Comparison with many other species with a much shorter dependency cycle had made the young of the species very vulnerable to predators. Social grouping also served as a collective protection to the species as a whole, although having the disadvantage of creating potential conflict between such social groupings.

The changes brought about by the breakdown of the family as a social unit, the institutional caring of the young, and an uncaring society in respect of the old, was in Anu's view, a dangerous pathway that humanity had pursued over the last decades. Not only had these changes taken away the means by which tradition and respect for the past was transferred from the old to the young, it had resulted in younger generations becoming dependant on influences that were outside the social unit, and where the thinking that "one size fits all" was accepted.

Development and diversity was consequently at a premium and contrary to the predictions of the Anunnaki when they initially genetically engineered the human species in the hope that one day humans would emerge as their worthy successors. The observable conflict between progressive scientific developments and the loss of stability in society was however an area of concern to Anu and one which he considered required attention by the World Council.

CHAPTER TWENTY NINE

Valencia like all cities across the world was in turmoil. Overnight the energy driven support systems that everyone took for granted had ceased to function. Computers which over the last millennium had become an essential component of all the service providers for society had suddenly stopped working bringing about complete chaos to the communications and transport services, and rendering most public service provision inoperable.

Air traffic control across the world had shutdown due to all computers, which normally automatically guided planes to and from their destinations, closed down, with the limited number of planes in the air at the point of shut-down being guided into land by a power source which the crew could not comprehend.

Intercity and city rail networks also ground to a halt with the automatic computer-controlled signalling system ceasing to function, resulting in numerous trains being marooned on stretches of track, and with passengers faced with the unenviable task of finding their way to their destination on foot.

The web monitor with access to the information highway, and which had become a feature of all homes and residences, just as the television set had been in the 20th century, was blank, with no signal, while mobile qPhones, so long the essential companion to both young and old alike, were silent with no signal and a blank screen.

Computerised check-out systems, now a feature of all retail stores, had also closed down, rendering the purchase of goods and services impossible.

Computerised production and packing facilities had also ceased to function as was the case with computerised manufacturing.

It was into this "dead" world that Sam woke on the morning of the Anunnaki's return, to discover a situation reminiscent of the happenings that had occurred when their plane was high jacked over the Atlantic, on its flight to Brisbane and when he had met Anu for the first time. Following his usual routine, Sam had showered only to discover the water was cold, visited the refrigerator for his customary glass of freshly squeezed orange juice, only to find that the refrigerator had no light came on when the door was open, as he was about to go out onto the balcony he noted the blank web screen in the corner of the lounge. Picking up his qPhone from the nearby table to call the energy suppliers he noted that his qPhone was also dead with no apparent signal denoting the web site that he normally used. It was then that the penny dropped, and he realised that he had lost all means of communication with the outside world.

Returning to the bedroom, and drawing back the curtains, he gently shook Margaret by the shoulders to wake her, saying "Wake up darling I think the Anunnaki have returned to earth."

CHAPTER THIRTY

Outside the building that housed the World Government Council, which by virtue of the failure of its electronic security systems, had been completely isolated from the outside world, with no means of entry or exit, chaos reigned. All the electronic aids and information systems that human society had developed and come to be dependent upon were suddenly inoperable having been decommissioned by the Anunnaki, and there was nothing that anyone could do to overcome this failure.

Inside the building with its now none functional security system, Daniel continued translating the telepathic thoughts of Anu into the spoken word. Words which held Dong Kurn lee and his colleagues of the Council spell bound.

Following a summary of their previous visits to earth, the on-going monitoring of their creation, and a brief summary of those factors that on previous visits to earth were seen by the Anunnaki as counterproductive to the development of humanity, Anu proceeded to identify in more detail his concerns relating to those characteristics that had developed within human society within relatively recent times, and which were at variance with the initial objectives of the Anunnaki when 450,000 years previously they had engineered the human genome and introduced it into the earth's primate species.

As Anu explained, the initial human genome was programmed to allow a gradual emergence of characteristics that, if allowed to develop, would eventually produce the next phase in human development. Regrettably from Ana's point of view relatively few individuals had exhibited such characteristics during the 450,000 years of human evolution, and the few who did, had through no fault of their own, frequently encountered an opposition from main stream society based on various ingrained beliefs, an apparent ingrained fear of the unknown, and a fear of any scientific development that involved humanity itself. Consequently, their influence on society as a whole was limited.

Development and scientific thinking had as a result only thrived in areas acceptable and useful to humanity of the time, and not as an alternative and long-term programme with specific aims.

This ad hoc development began with the invention of the "wheel" as a means of transport on land, the boat as a means of transport on water, and the aeroplane as a means of air travel, culminating in the computerisation and/or electronic control of practically all forms of transport.

Since this visit was the first by the Anunnaki since the establishment of a World Government, bringing home this most important concept of assistance in the development of humanity to those members sitting in the Council Chamber was Anu's objective, and as he had indicated, was the reason why the electronic dependant world of 2112 had been "shut down" to illustrate the vulnerability of this dependability.

Over the millennia, humanity had developed numerous artistic, mechanical and electronic aids to a high level of sophistication, resulting in it becoming not only less dependent on its own ability to survive, but becoming the only species inhabiting the planet that had come dependent on "outside aids" in its functioning in everyday life, and in some instances, for its very survival.

This dependency, according to Anu, had not been the intention of the Anunnaki, since in keeping with the evolutionary pattern of all species, they had anticipated that with the passage of time the gradual evolution of humans would eventually lead to individuals possessing some, if not all, those characteristics which their "creators" had implanted in the human genome, and equally important that such individuals would have the wisdom to use those gifts as intended. In Anu's opinion it was regrettable that with very few exceptions, of which Daniel was one, this development had not occurred, although human history was scattered with individuals who had recognisable special gifts and qualities as a consequence of the random combinations of DNA.

Again using Daniel as his mouth-piece, Anu proceeded to outline what the Anunnaki expected of the World Government over the next millennia in terms of ensuring that humanity would not founder on its own developments but develop along the lines originally envisaged by the Anunnaki.

In doing this the Anunnaki were effectively prescribing "Commandments" to humanity similar to those that, according to ancient scriptures, had been delivered to various societies over the passage of time, and as exemplified by the "tablets" containing the Ten Commandments delivered to the Jews at Mount Sinai, and the writings of the Koran.

Paramount was the need for a reappraisal of the system of Type 1 and Type 2 "Reservations". While it was accepted that Type 1 safeguarded society as a whole from criminals and evil doers, Type 2 had effectively isolated those members of society who had not agreed with the developments initiated by their "modern" colleagues in main stream society.

In Anu's view the inhabitants of Type 2 reservations represented the bed-rock of human evolution up to the present time, in so far as the social nature of humanity had been preserved   and since humans by their primate origins were essentially a social species, this characteristic should be fostered and preserved and reintroduced into mainstream society. As he further emphasised, Daniel was a product of a Type 2 reservation, and without his assistance as a "mouthpiece" communication between the Anunnaki and members of the World Government would not have been possible.

The second issue related to the propagation of the species in main line society, where invitro fertilization and invitro embryology had replaced reproductive sex, and the development of the resulting embryo in the female's womb. Although such techniques had relieved the female of this responsibility and allowed her a life-style compatible to that of her male partner, it had encouraged same-sex relationships, with children becoming a kind of "status" symbol cared and educated by the State against a background of social engineering.

In-vitro fertilization and in-vitro embryology clinics worldwide, while having a role to play a century previous, had ostensibly modified and over-reached their role, resulting in normal propagation of the species being restricted to those who had chosen to live in type 2 reservations.

The Anunnaki had serious concerns at this development and viewed the on-going procreation of the species currently restricted to the inhabitants of Type 2 Reservations as an essential change for the future.

The third area of concern related to the dependency of humanity on electronic aids, which in very many areas had significantly affected the development of communicative skills in the young, had significantly affected both their education and the acquisition of skills, and of even greater importance had greatly reduced most forms of mental stimulation.

Mental stimulation of the human brain was in Anu's view an essential component to the development of the brain, thought processes, communicative skills and brain power. This stimulation had over the decades been reduced by the adoption of technology that made life easier.

There was, as Anu emphasised, latent power in the brain of all humans, which allowed for such powers as extra sensory perception, psychokinetic, telekinetic, psychoportation, parapsychology and genetic memory abilities to develop, and which under prevailing conditions had very little chance of doing so, since an enormous amount of time and money had been invested in creating alternatives such as artificial brains, the q-pod and similar devices which performed most of the basic functions of the brain and which were used extensively by humans in their every day existence.

Daniel, as Anu emphasised, had miraculously through a random combination of genes, developed these mental powers which had been initially introduced into the human genome by the Anunnaki some 450,000 years previous. These powers had now enabled him to communicate with his creators and pass on their message to human kind.

These three commandments were in Anu's opinion an essential component of humanity's future, and unless complied with would result in the Anunnaki disabling all electronic activity on earth. In the meantime the current blockade would be lifted on his return to the planet Nibiru, but would be re-introduced if significant progress had not been achieved by his next visit to earth.

With these words, Anu using his psychoportation abilities, disappeared leaving an exhausted Daniel slumped in front of the world governance members. At the same time the electronic security systems and

137

communication systems sprang to life, and once again the creators of human kind had delivered their message and returned to the heavens.

Would their commandments be heeded? Or will compliance be only possible by force? Only time will tell.

www.ingramcontent.com/pod-product-compliance
Lightning Source LLC
Chambersburg PA
CBHW030131260626
47156CB00008B/2900